Something to Talk About

What Reviewers Say About Ronica Black's Work

A Love that Leads to Home

"If you love a slow-burn romance where the characters are carefully dancing around each other while being incredibly adorable, this story is for you. It was an emotional read for me, and if you want a good heart-wrenching story, read it." —*Hsinju's Lit Log*

Freedom to Love

"This is a great book. The police drama keeps you enthralled throughout but what I found captivating was the growing affection between the two main characters. Although they are both very different women, you find yourself holding your breath, hoping that they will find a way to be together." —*Lesbian Reading Room*

The Practitioner

"*The Practitioner* by Ronica Black is the angsty sort of romance that I can easily get lost in. I wanted to fill a tub and bathe in all the feelings. Hell, if I had one of those fancy, waterproof Kindles, I just might have."—*Lesbian Review*

"The beginning of this novel captured my attention from the rather luscious description of a pint of Guinness. I cannot tell a lie, I almost immediately wanted to be drinking it. …The first scene with the practitioner also pulled me in, making me sit up and pay attention to what was happening on the digital page. The relationship was like a low simmering fire, frequently doused by either Johnnie's personal angst, or Elaine's. This book was an overall enjoyable read and one which I would recommend to people wanting characters who practically breathe off the page."—*Library Thing*

Snow Angel

"A beautifully written, passionate and romantic novella." —*SunsetXCocktail*

"*Snow Angel* is a novella, and it flies by. It draws characters and scenes in large strokes, and it's good fun if you'd like a quick read that's particularly escapist."—*The Lesbrary*

Under Her Wing

"From the start Ronica Black had me. I loved everything about this story, from the emotional intensity to the amazingly hot sex scenes. The emotion between them is so real and tear jerking at times. And the love scenes are phenomenal. I feel I'm raving—but I enjoyed it that much. Highly recommended."—*Kitty Kat's Book Review Blog*

***"Emily" in* Women of the Dark Streets**

"A darkly disturbing brush with questionable magic that leads to an astounding one-eighty-degree turnaround after an apparent attempt at suicide. Mindboggling!"—*Rainbow Book Reviews*

The Seeker

"Stalkers, child kidnappers and murderers all collide in this fast-paced, dual-plotted novel. This is not Black's first novel, and readers can only hope it will not be her last."—*Lambda Literary Review*

"Ronica Black's books just keep getting stronger and stronger. ...This is such a tightly written plot-driven novel that readers will find themselves glued to the pages and ignoring phone calls. *The Seeker* is a great read, with an exciting plot, great characters, and great sex."—*Just About Write*

Flesh and Bone—*Lambda Literary Award Finalist*

"Ronica Black handles a traditional range of lesbian fantasies with gusto and sincerity. The reader wants to know these women as well as they come to know each other. When Black's characters ignore their realistic fears to follow their passion, this reader admires their chutzpah and cheers them on. ...These stories make good bedtime reading, and could lead to sweet dreams. Read them and see."—*Erotica Revealed*

Chasing Love

"Ronica Black's writing is fluid, and lots of dialogue makes this a fast read. If you like steamy erotica with intense sexual situations, you'll like *Chasing Love*."—*Queer Magazine Online*

Hearts Aflame

"Sleek storytelling and terrific characters are the backbone of Ronica Black's third and best novel, *Hearts Aflame*. Prepare to hop on for an emotional ride with this thrilling story of love in the outback. …Along with the romance of Krista and Rae, the secondary storylines such as Krista's fear of horses and an uncle suffering from Alzheimer's are told with depth and warmth. Black also draws in the reader by utilizing the weather as a metaphor for the sexual and emotional tension in all the storylines. Wonderful storytelling and rich characterization make this a high recommendation."—*Lambda Literary Review*

"I like the author's writing style and she tells a good story. I was drawn in quickly and didn't lose interest at all. Black paints a great picture with her words and I was able to feel like I was sitting around the camp fire with the characters." —*C-Spot Reviews*

Wild Abandon—*Lambda Literary Award Finalist*

"Black is a master at teasing the reader with her use of domination and desire. Black's first novel, *In Too Deep*, was a finalist for a 2005 Lammy. …With *Wild Abandon*, the author continues her winning ways, writing like a seasoned pro. This is one romance I will not soon forget."—*Books to Watch Out For*

"This sequel to Ronica Black's debut novel, *In Too Deep*, is an electrifying thriller. The author's development as a fine storyteller shines with this tightly written story. …[The mystery] keeps the story charged—never unraveling or leading us to a predictable conclusion. More than once I gasped in surprise at the dark and twisted paths this book took."—*Curve*

"Black has managed to create two very sensual and compelling women. The backstory is intriguing, original, and quite well-developed. Yet, it doesn't detract from the primary premise of the novel—it is a sexually-charged romance about two very different and guarded women. Black carries the reader along at such a rapid pace that the rise and fall of each climactic moment successfully creates that suspension of disbelief which the reader seeks."—*Midwest Book Review*

In Too Deep—*Lambda Literary Award Finalist*

"Ronica Black's debut novel *In Too Deep* has everything from nonstop action and intriguing well developed characters to steamy erotic love scenes. From the opening scenes where Black plunges the reader headfirst into the story to the explosive unexpected ending, *In Too Deep* has what it takes to rise to the top. Black has a winner with *In Too Deep*, one that will keep the reader turning the pages until the very last one."—*Independent Gay Writer*

"…an exciting, page turning read, full of mystery, sex, and suspense."—*MegaScene*

"…a challenging murder mystery—sections of this mixed-genre novel are hot, hot, hot. Black juggles the assorted elements of her first book with assured pacing and estimable panache." —*Q Syndicate*

"Black's characterization is skillful, and the sexual chemistry surrounding the three major characters is palpable and definitely hot-hot-hot…if you're looking for a solid read with ample amounts of eroticism and a red herring or two you're sure to find *In Too Deep* a satisfying read."—*L Word Literature*

"Every time the reader has a handle on what's happening, Black throws in a curve, successfully devising a good mystery. The romance and sex add a special gift to the package rounding out the story for a totally satisfying read."—*Just About Write*

By the Author

In Too Deep
Deeper
Wild Abandon
Hearts Aflame
Flesh and Bone
The Seeker
Chasing Love
Conquest
Wholehearted
The Midnight Room
Snow Angel
The Practitioner
Freedom to Love
Under Her Wing
Private Passion
Dark Euphoria
The Last Seduction
Olivia's Awakening
A Love That Leads to Home
Passion's Sweet Surrender
A Turn of Fate
Watching Over Her
The Business of Pleasure
Something to Talk About

Something to Talk About

by

Ronica Black

2022

SOMETHING TO TALK ABOUT

ISBN 13: 978-1-63679-114-2

This Trade Paperback Original Is Published By
Bold Strokes Books, Inc.
P.O. Box 249
Valley Falls, NY 12185

First Edition: May 2022

Credits
Editor: Cindy Cresap
Production Design: Susan Ramundo
Cover Design By Tammy Seidick

Acknowledgments

Thank you to everyone at BSB for making this book possible.

Chapter One

The early evening air was cool and crisp as Corey Durand knelt to examine another pumpkin. The rind was smooth and undamaged, the green color just beginning to change to orange. She turned it so the other side had equal time in the sun, and then moved down the row, doing the same to the others, her border collie mix, Whip, by her side. The pumpkins were growing fast now, and it wouldn't be long before they were ready to sell. She rose and adjusted the bill of her ball cap as she called out to her ranch hands across the patch. "They're looking good over here, guys. What about you?"

Ryan gave her a thumbs-up from near the fence line and Grey walked over to her, spitting sunflower seed shells out of the side of her mouth as she approached.

"They'll be ready for harvest soon," she said in her no-nonsense gravelly voice.

"I'm hoping so," Corey said. They studied the vast patch. The bits of orange rind peeking through the green was set off by the setting sun, and Corey once again thought how lucky she was to have her ranch and witness such beauty. The pumpkin patch was a new addition to the ranch, but, as today proved, it only added to the beauty of her land.

"You're happy, ain't ya?" Grey asked with a smirk.

"That I am."

"Yeah, you got that look again."

"Can't help it. Sometimes I think I'm the luckiest woman in the world."

"I know you think so."

"I do. I mean, look at all this." She spread her arms and they stared off beyond the patch to the two barns, the stables, the old silo, and the house. It didn't look like much to most people, but to Corey, it was everything.

"Most people would only see the work needed to be done and the big bucks offered to you by land developers."

Corey removed her hat and scratched her brow. "Yeah, well, I'm not most people. This place is my home. Always has been, always will be."

"I know. You ain't got to tell me twice."

Corey chuckled and placed her khaki Durand Farms cap back on her head.

They headed through the patch back toward the main part of the ranch while Ryan brought up the rear and Whip took off ahead of them to sniff more growing pumpkins.

"You really think this little venture of yours is gonna pay off?" Grey asked as she lumbered along next to her.

"Hell, yes," Corey said. "It's almost fall and who doesn't love pumpkins?"

"You gotta point there," Grey said.

Corey knelt and checked a larger pumpkin. It was going to make for a nice jack-o'-lantern come time.

"Money's tight. I had to get creative."

"I understand."

She grinned at her. "Of course, I coulda just gotten rid of you. Save me a bundle."

Grey snickered and spit. "I'd like to see you try and run this place without me."

"Wouldn't be that hard. Ryan's coming along nicely."

"He's a child."

"Hey, I'm nineteen!" Ryan called out.

Corey laughed. "See, he's nineteen. A big boy now."

"You guys are hilarious," Ryan said.

"Seriously though, you aren't really considering retiring on me, are you?" Corey asked as they continued to walk through the patch.

Grey worked her jaw as if in deep thought. "Maggie's wanting me to. Says I'm too old to be messing around here."

"She just wants you home with her." Corey rested her hand on her shoulder. "Can't say I blame her. You're good to have around."

"Don't get all lovey-dovey on me now," she said. "Doesn't suit you."

Corey chuckled. "I can't help it. You're just so lovable."

"Shit," she said, causing Corey to laugh again.

They were nearing the exit to the patch when Ryan called out from behind.

"Hey, you guys, look!"

Corey and Grey turned toward the commotion. Corey stopped dead in her tracks. She blinked to make sure that what she was seeing was real.

A little girl was crawling through the wooden fence line. And when she entered the patch, she immediately ran to a pumpkin and tried to lift it off the ground, vine still attached.

"What the hell?" Corey said.

"Well, I'll be goddamned," Grey said.

Corey and Grey headed toward the child, who looked to be no more than four or five years old. She was intently focused on lifting the pumpkin, her golden hair shining in the setting sun.

"Where in the world did she come from?" Corey asked, quickly scanning the grounds for an accompanying adult. But there was no one. Just the house in the distance, the one that sat just off her property, the one no one had lived in for more than ten years.

"I don't know," Grey said.

Whip ran up to the girl and inspected her, but the girl had no interest.

Corey approached, more confused than ever. She had forty acres and rarely did people stop by unexpected. Those that did came to ride the horses she boarded or to purchase goat milk from her numerous pygmy goats. But no one had ever been out to this side of the ranch before. Especially not an unaccompanied child.

Ryan pulled off his cowboy hat and scratched his head, giving Corey a look that let her know he was just as confused as she was.

"You've never seen her before?" she asked him.

He shook his head.

"Hello," Corey said as she walked up to the little girl and placed her hand on Whip's head.

The girl didn't even look up, she just kept playing with the pumpkin. Trying to yank it from the vine.

Corey looked to Grey, and Ryan and tried again.

"Hi." She knelt in front of her, hoping to get her attention. "What's your name?"

It didn't work. The little girl seemed to be intently focused on the pumpkin.

"Here," Corey said, loosening a smaller one for her. She handed it over. "Take this one."

The little girl finally raised her eyes, but only looked at Corey fleetingly before she homed in on her prize. She took it immediately and held it close, turning it over and over in her tiny hands.

"Do you like that?" Corey asked. Maybe the child was just shy. She could understand that. She had some difficulty with shyness as well.

The little girl kept examining her pumpkin. Soon she moved on to another small one and tried to loosen it. Corey helped her and handed it over. Once again, the girl took it without a word. Then she straightened, one pumpkin in each hand, and headed for the fence line.

"What, she don't talk?" Grey said.

"Doesn't look like it," Corey said, watching her. "Ryan, open the gate for her."

"You're letting her go?" Grey asked.

"We're going to follow her."

Ryan scrambled to the gate and opened it for the child. Then they followed her through the high grass toward the house in the distance. The little girl walked a little funny, pushing up on her toes with each step. Corey found it endearing. She'd never seen anyone walk that way before.

They weren't a few seconds into their walk when they heard a scream and then a woman calling out. Suddenly, Corey could see a small group of people clamoring around the back of the house and running toward the field.

"Looks like we found her home," Grey said.

"Looks like it," Corey said.

A woman bolted into the lead as she caught sight of the little girl, and she flat-out sprinted before collapsing in front of her and embracing her tightly.

"Oh, my God," she said. "Oh, my God." She was breathless and tears were streaming down her face. "Oh, Laken, I was so worried. Oh, dear God, I was so scared." She continued to hug the little girl but got little in response. It didn't seem to surprise her.

The woman finally glanced up at Corey and her crew. She stood and tried haphazardly to smooth her long blond hair away from her face. She cleared her throat and pegged them with a curious stare.

"Are you the ones who found her?" she asked.

Corey glanced at Grey and Ryan. "Well, actually, ma'am, she sort of found us."

The woman blinked rapidly. "What do you mean?"

Corey explained. "She came upon my pumpkin patch just back a ways. And we happened to be out there."

"So you let her pick pumpkins?"

Corey stiffened. "Well, yes. It was all she was about. So I let her have a couple."

The woman sighed. "Great. Now that's all she'll be wanting to do."

Grey grumbled something and spit. She turned a little as if she was ready to return to the ranch.

"I'm sorry," Corey said, a little perturbed by her manner. "What would you have me do? We didn't know who she was or where she came from. She wouldn't talk—"

"I know." She held up a hand and then rubbed her brow in obvious frustration. "I—she's nonverbal. Look, thank you for bringing her home. I apologize for any trouble she caused."

"No trouble," Corey said. Whip hurried up to the woman and gave her his best welcome with quick licks of her hand and shakes of his tail. The woman glanced at him but seemed too perturbed to pay much attention.

"Whip, come." He returned to Corey's side, and they all watched as the woman tried to take a pumpkin from Laken in order to take her by the hand, but Laken cried and jerked away.

"Fine, you can carry your pumpkins," she said. She gave Corey and her friends a forced smile. "Well, I need to be getting back to the movers."

Corey wanted to ask her about the move. About when she'd bought the house and who all was living there. She hadn't had neighbors in a very long time, and to be honest, she wasn't looking forward to it now. She liked her privacy. Liked her peace.

"Okay, then," Corey said. "I'm Corey, by the way. And this is Grey and Ryan. And this," she said, pointing downward, "is Whip."

The woman seemed flustered. Almost…irritated. "Yes, of course. I'm Brin. And this is Laken." But she didn't step forward to offer her hand. And she didn't hold eye contact for much longer. "Well, I really need to be getting back."

"We won't hold you up then," Corey said.

With that, Brin turned and walked away, following Laken who carried her two little pumpkins in her fists.

"What a weird woman," Ryan said as they began to head back to the ranch.

"Rude as all get-out," Grey mumbled.

"Give her a break," Corey said, trying to understand the woman's demeanor. "She was obviously stressed over losing the child."

"Even so," said Grey. "Manners is manners."

Corey said nothing, wondering again about Brin and Laken. Were they alone or did one of the others at the house reside with them?

Why am I so curious?

"She's a nice enough little girl," Ryan said. "Wonder why she doesn't talk."

"Maybe because we're strangers," Corey said, once again trying to explain. She wasn't sure why she was sticking up for her new neighbors and making excuses for them. Maybe to comfort herself somehow, the thought of having rude or unusual neighbors too much for her to handle at the moment.

"Maybe," said Ryan. "Or maybe like Grey said. They're just rude."

"Either way," Grey mumbled. "You got yourself some new neighbors to contend with."

"Yeah," said Corey, staring into the setting sun. "I know."

"So, you can kiss your peace and quiet good-bye."

Corey squinted at her. "Why do you say that?"

Grey laughed. "Because, Durand. That little girl just found herself a whole new playground and you're the king of the castle."

"She won't bother me," Corey said, hoping Grey was wrong. "She's probably getting an earful right now about venturing onto my property."

Ryan kicked at a rock with his boot-covered foot. "I'm with Grey," he said. "She'll be back."

"You're wrong," Corey said, glancing back at Brin's house. "Her mother will see to it that she doesn't come back."

Grey looked at her as they reentered the pumpkin patch. "Who said I was just talking about the kid?"

Corey blinked, and once again Grey laughed, leaving Corey more confused than ever.

CHAPTER TWO

Laken," Breana said, her voice so weak she could hardly speak.

Brin gripped her dying sister's hand and held it to her face, waiting.

"Take care of...her."

A tear slipped down Brin's face as she stared into her eyes. Eyes that were so much like her own, now void of vibrancy and a zest for life. Eyes that were seconds from extinguishing forever.

"I will," Brin choked.

"Swear," Breana said. Her pale forehead creased beneath the bandana that covered her balding head. Her lips were cracked and her cheeks sunken. She was a far cry from the woman she once was, and yet Brin thought she was still just as beautiful.

"I swear," Brin said, trying to hold back more tears. "I'll love and protect her with my life. You have my word."

Breana closed her eyes and took another ragged breath. "Mom and Dad...too old. Too much for them."

"I know."

She opened her eyes. "I'm sorry," she said. "To leave you."

"It's okay," Brin said, this time choking on the rising tears.

"Laken," she said again. "I love her. Always."

"I know."

"Make sure...she knows."

Brin nodded and touched her forehead. "I will."

"Love you," she said and closed her eyes again.

She took one last long breath and stilled.

Brin squeezed her hand. "I love you, too."

Brin awoke with a gasp and sat up in bed. Tears streaked her face and she wiped them away as she scanned her environment. For a moment, she was at a loss as to where she was. But as she saw the walls with the peeling wallpaper, the hardwood floors that needed refinishing, and the secondhand furniture she'd just found at the local Goodwill, she remembered that she was in her home, in the small northern Arizona town of Utopia. A place she'd never dreamed she'd end up.

"But here I am." She pushed back her covers and rose, sliding her feet into her worn bedroom slippers. The floor creaked as she walked into the kitchen, and she hugged herself from the morning chill. Utopia was a lot cooler than Phoenix and she'd have to invest in some winter pajamas sometime soon as her boxer shorts and T-shirt were no longer warm enough.

I hope Laken is warm enough.

After quickly starting a pot of coffee, she walked the short distance to Laken's room. She found her asleep in her little bed, all curled up with her white stuffed whale named Charlie. Laken rarely went anywhere inside the house without Charlie. And she definitely didn't sleep without him. Brin knew one night soon she'd have to take the whale from her as she slept, just so she could wash it. As it was, ol' Charlie was looking pretty dingy and worse for wear.

Brin tucked the stuffed animal closer to her, along with her covers, and left her to sleep. Then she headed for the hallway where she turned on the heat. To her great relief, it kicked on, and she could feel the nip in the air begin to subside.

She made her way back to the kitchen where she poured herself a full cup of coffee. She sat at the small kitchen table and stirred in her stevia and took a nice, long sip. It immediately hit the spot, and in no time at all, the chill in her bones was gone.

Thank God the heat works.

Things had been hit-or-miss with the house so far, but overall she was grateful. She'd taken what savings she'd had and the profit from selling her townhouse to buy the old place. Her folks had considered it a risky move, but for her it was perfect. She'd always dreamt of leaving Phoenix for the north, and with the death of Breana and her now legal guardianship of Laken, she thought it a perfect time to make her move. Laken needed a fresh start. Hell, she'd needed a fresh start. After the dramatic end to her last relationship, and the fiasco that had happened in regard to her job, the quiet life in Utopia was looking and sounding pretty darn good. But she figured almost any place other than Phoenix would after what she'd been through. Thankfully though, she'd ended up here. And with a little work…okay, a lot of work, the house would make a great home for her and Laken, everyone else be damned.

I am grateful.

She glanced around, noticed the water stain on the kitchen ceiling and cringed.

I am, I am, I am.

She reminded herself that things were going as good as could be expected so far. Thankfully, Laken usually slept the night through. The loss of her mother, somehow, not disturbing her sleep very often. She'd had a total of two nightmares since Breana's death, but being nonverbal, she'd been unable to tell Brin whether or not they'd been about her mother. Brin suspected they had been, having to rock her to sleep in her arms on both occasions, which in itself was unusual. And there were the few occasions when Laken would crawl up in her lap, along with the picture of her mother, wanting to snuggle. Brin would hold her and tell her a story or two about Breana and Laken would usually fall asleep or she'd eventually push her away and get down, off to her world of silence and make-believe. Laken wasn't crazy about affection, and she sometimes fought Brin on being held. But seeing as how the doctors were telling her she was on the spectrum, it didn't surprise Brin any. Laken had always been fiercely independent. She did things her own way and lived in her own little world. Some days it was a miracle if Brin could get her to interact at all. So when she did crawl up next to her, or allow Brin to hold her, it was all Brin could do not to close her eyes and thank the stars above.

Laken was special and raising her was going to be a challenge. But Brin wouldn't have it any other way. She loved her more than life itself and had always had a soft spot for her, little quirks and all. And Laken loved her, too. Next to Breana, Brin was the only one Laken would give the time of day. So, it only made sense that Brin would take on the care for her.

Brin sipped more coffee and stared out the windows of the nook, beyond the tall grass to the ranch behind her. Dawn had just broken, but she could see someone out in the field, apparently walking in the pumpkin patch. She could just make out some hints of round orange as the person moved about, kneeling and inspecting them every so often.

"I wonder if that's Corey."

She was both surprised at having remembered her name and also surprised that she was so curious. Still, she kept watching, convinced that the lean figure in the jeans and khaki ball cap was indeed Corey, the woman she'd met the day before.

Brin continued to sip her coffee with her eyes trained on her new neighbor. She supposed it was nice to live next door to lesbians, as it was always nice to have other gays close by. But for some reason she was uneasy about living next to Corey.

Is it because she's so attractive?

The admission made her cringe once again. She'd seen the woman all of five minutes, spoken to her very briefly, and she'd noticed her attractiveness. But yes, that was it. She was uneasy because Corey was attractive. And trouble with another woman was the last thing she needed.

She rubbed her forehead and fixed her eyes on her coffee mug, trying to convince herself that Corey didn't really do it for her. For one thing, Corey was older, she had gray hair at her temples and crow's-feet at her eyes. Brin had never dated anyone older than her and she pegged Corey for her late forties, possibly early fifties. And then there was her masculinity. Brin had only ever dated feminine women. Not because she had anything against anyone else, it was just who she was drawn to.

But now there was Corey. Her new neighbor. Her new *attractive* neighbor.

She looked back up and saw Corey crossing the patch. She watched her walk, watched her tug down on the bill of her ball cap. Watched her long, lean arms sway and the gentle sashay of her tight-looking backside.

The woman looked good in worn jeans. She'd give her that.

Brin sighed and drank more coffee. It didn't matter how good-looking Corey was, the fact of the matter was that the other woman, the one whose name she couldn't remember, was probably her partner. Therefore, Corey was off limits. And it was just as well. She'd promised herself no women and no drama. She had Laken to focus on now and she was all that mattered.

Still, I can look, can't I?

She shook her head.

No.

She closed her eyes and resigned herself to a life of possible celibacy. Or at least until Laken was good and settled.

Yes, but when will that be?

She opened her eyes and found Corey to be gone.

Thank God.

She couldn't seem to rely on her own self-discipline. She'd been in the house less than twenty-four hours and she was already thinking about the damn neighbor.

Was she that impossible? Or was it simply because she'd had very little in the way of love and affection thanks to the last year with Tracy?

It must be the latter. Yes, it was definitely the latter. Tracy had shut off from her and that was why she was so starved for female attention. That had to be it.

The floor squeaked and she saw Laken walking into the room. She had a fist in her eye, wiping away the sleep, and she was walking on her toes, just as she always did. Toe-walking was a symptom of those on the spectrum and the doctors had told her not to worry about it. Still, she wondered if it hurt her to toe-walk so much.

"Good morning, sunshine," Brin said with a smile. She rose to pick her up, but Laken refused, choosing instead to take her by the hand.

"Oh, okay. Where are we going?"

Laken led her to the pantry and pointed at the Cheerios. Then she led her to the fridge and pointed at the milk.

This was the mealtime ritual. Laken would pull her to whatever it was she wanted and point. And very rarely did she stray from what she usually wanted.

"Okay," Brin said, grabbing the box of cereal and the carton of milk. Laken walked to the table and waited for Brin to lift her into her booster seat. Brin brought the goods to the table and did just that, and then poured the dry cereal into a small bowl and poured the milk into a sippy cup.

Laken never ate the cereal in milk. She preferred things crunchy and easy to grip with her fingers. She took a fistful of Cheerios and began to eat.

Brin refilled her coffee and joined her at the table. The rising sun shone on Laken's lemon hair and lit up her beautiful light green eyes. She looked like an angel sitting there eating her breakfast, wrapped in the halo of golden light. Her Blue's Clues pajamas looked cute on her, but Brin reminded herself she needed to buy her warmer ones today. She wondered if Laken would be willing to pick some out and whether or not she'd fight her on wearing them.

"Laken, are you cold?"

Laken didn't look at her. She just kept eating and swinging her bare feet.

Brin surmised she probably wasn't as cold as she was because Breana had kept their house at a lower temperature than she did year-round. The current temperature was probably perfect for Laken, if not a little warm.

Even so, fall was fast approaching and no doubt the first snow. They needed to be prepared.

"We're gonna go shopping today, okay?"

Laken slurped at her milk.

"Okay, Lake?"

Laken looked at her very briefly and returned to her cereal. Brin smiled.

"Thank you."

She always thanked her when she made eye contact, for each time was a victory, no matter how small.

Now, she only had to figure out how to win some bigger ones.

CHAPTER THREE

Corey pulled her old Chevy truck into a parking space just outside of Flick's Hardware. She removed her ball cap, ran a hand through her short hair, and replaced the hat on her head. Then she climbed out and slammed the heavy door closed.

"Mabel," she said as she tugged on her bill.

Mabel Ashbury nodded in greeting as she walked by, arms full of groceries.

"Need any help?" Corey asked.

"No, thank you, Corrina." She smiled and Corey returned it, even if the use of her given name almost made her cringe. But folks around town, the older folks in particular, still remembered her as little Corrina. The tomboy with the beautiful name. A name she despised, even if her mother had given it out of love after her great-grandmother. It just didn't seem to fit Corey.

It was too…well, feminine.

Corey watched Mabel cross to her car and put away her groceries. Once she was sure she was okay, she headed inside the store and slapped her hand down on the worn counter. "Flick, how the hell are ya?"

Flick Haywood popped up from the shelves behind the counter and grinned.

"Well, Corey Durand. What a nice surprise."

Corey laughed. "It's not that much of a surprise."

"I haven't seen you in what seems like ages. Hear you been shopping over at the new hardware store down the highway."

"Not as much as you think."

"Ha." He waved her off. "You're all a bunch of traitors. The whole lot of you. Shoulda known it the second I heard that gargantuan crapatorium of a store was going up. Shoulda cashed my goods in and split. Headed down to Mexico where my brother is. Living in paradise, he says. Son of a bitch." He rounded the counter and opened the standing cooler to pull out a cold bottle of Pepsi. He handed it to Corey.

"Open that, will you? My bones is acting up something fierce."

She twisted off the cap and watched as he heartily slurped.

"Yeah, that giant shit store's gonna be the death of me. You wait and see." He burped softly and then refocused on Corey, almost as if he'd forgotten she was there.

"What can I do you for, Corey? Something big? Something small?"

"I need a new drill bit."

"Ah. Something I have." He turned and swung his long white braid down the back of his leather vest. He led the way down the correct aisle and Corey just smiled, already knowing the store inside and out. Why he was choosing to escort her was beyond her. Maybe it was a new customer service bonus seeing as how he was worried about the big chain store taking him out.

"Here we are," he said, motioning like a spokesmodel. "All the drill bits you could possibly need." He sank a gnarled-looking hand into the small front pocket of his leather vest. Faded peace sign patches dotted the front.

He seemed to be waiting for Corey to choose her drill bit, as his bright eyes were watching her closely.

She quickly scanned the goods and found what she needed. She held it up as if she'd found a hidden treasure.

"Here it is."

"Ah, perfect," he said, taking it from her. "Did you need anything else? Anything at all?" His face looked hopeful, his bushy white eyebrows matching the white of his beard.

Corey could feel the quiet desperation coming off him. It was like an invisible mist, and she suddenly felt solely responsible for the survival of his store.

"You know I might as well get a new drill, too."

"A new drill?" His eyes lit up like a slot machine.

Corey nodded and threw up her hands. "Might as well."

She followed Flick down the aisle to the drills and began looking. Flick was talking to her, giving his opinion on each one, but Corey wasn't paying much attention. She knew he needed to talk so she let him. But truth was, she already knew exactly which drill she wanted. She'd been wanting it for a while and now felt like as good a time as any to splurge and buy it.

She pointed when he'd finished his report. He seemed pleased with her choice and he tried to grab it off the shelf to carry it, but his hands were obviously hurting him, and she didn't want him to have to set down his drink just for her when she was perfectly capable of carrying it herself.

"Here, let me, Flick. You've got your drink."

He seemed thankful for the help and didn't argue with her any.

She carried the drill to the front counter and waited. Flick came ambling after her, still carrying the drill bit. He proudly set it on the counter and got busy ringing up her purchase.

The bell above the door chimed as Miley Roberts walked in, looking every bit the debutant she still considered herself to be.

"Well, hello, hello," she said to the two of them.

Flick looked up and gave a polite nod. "Mrs. Roberts."

"That's Ms. now, Flick. David and I split two years ago, remember?"

Remember? How could anyone forget? Their divorce may as well have made the front pages of the newspaper it was so big and dramatic. And Miley? She got half of David's fortune despite never having lifted a finger to help with his business. And she wasn't about to let anyone forget it.

"God knows I earned that respect at the very least," she said. Her gaze settled on Corey, and instead of the blatant contempt she usually showed toward her, her overly made-up face lit up, much like Flick's had earlier. Anxiety flooded Corey as she wondered why.

"Corey Durand. Just the woman I wanted to see." She reached for Corey's hand and held it in her own as if they were the world's oldest friends.

"And why is that?" Corey asked.

"Because I want you to come to my party, silly." She squeaked as she laughed. She must've seen the downright shock on Corey's face because she continued before Corey could question her.

"As I'm sure you know, I'm having a fall fiesta this year and I'd love it if you'd come!"

Corey started to protest, but Miley wouldn't have it. "Now, before you say no, I want you to think good and hard about it. You see, I heard it through the grapevine that you're growing pumpkins this season and I could use some at my little get-together."

"What about Joy Harper?"

"Oh, Joy Harper's pumpkins suck." She squeaked again. "Don't tell her I said that, of course."

"Of course," Corey said, knowing they must've had a falling out.

"So, what do you say? You come and bring some of your pumpkins? It'll be great advertising for your pumpkin patch."

Corey mulled it over for a second, considering the offer. It was true that she despised Miley Roberts more than most people and that parties in general weren't her thing. But the promise of putting a good word out about her pumpkin patch was tempting. Very tempting.

"Okay," she said, winning herself a quick series of jumps and squeaks from Miley.

"Oh, goodie! Okay, I'll call you with all the deets."

Corey nodded and took her bag from Flick who looked like he was begging for her to stay so he wouldn't have to be alone with Miley. But Corey figured she'd done enough good deeds for the day.

She tipped her hat at Miley and thanked Flick.

Then she headed outside back into the sunshine.

As she squinted into the sunlight, she caught sight of her new neighbor struggling to start her car. Corey thought about moving on, about letting someone else worry about helping her, but she just couldn't do it. It wasn't in her to be impolite and not help. And what was it that was causing her to second-guess her helpful nature anyway? The woman hadn't done anything to her. Other than be a little rude. But she'd had good reason. She'd been worried about the little girl.

I'm being ridiculous. Of course I'll help.

Corey walked over to her and stood just outside the driver's door of the small sedan.

"Car trouble?"

The woman, whose name she remembered was Brin, glanced over at her quickly, then did a double take.

"She won't start."

She tried again but got nothing.

Corey leaned on the car and took a look inside. She could see Laken, the little girl from the day before, sitting in the back in her car seat.

"Sounds like it could be your battery. When's the last time you had a new one?"

Brin blew out a breath. "It's not my battery."

Corey blinked, waiting for more. She got nothing.

"Okay. Any idea what it could be then?"

She shook her head in obvious frustration. "I don't know. Christ. I just know it's not the battery."

Corey swallowed, almost afraid to ask. "How do you know that?"

Brin whipped her head around to glare at her. "Because I just replaced it like, I don't know, two years ago."

"Ah," Corey said.

"What?"

"You from Phoenix?"

"What does that matter?"

"The heat eats up the batteries. Especially if your car's been sitting a while."

Brin clamped her mouth closed.

"Has your car been sitting?" Corey carefully asked.

Brin hit the steering wheel with the heel of her hand.

"Some. Damn it. I don't have time for this."

"If you want, I can give you a jump."

Brin looked at her as if she were sizing her up. "That's okay. We can manage." She looked back at Laken.

Corey took the opportunity to cross to her truck to search for the jumper cables anyway. To her dismay, she realized she didn't have them. She'd loaned them out to Ryan.

Corey returned to Brin, who'd popped the hood and was inspecting the insides.

"Sorry, I don't have the cables. But I can do you one better and give you a lift over to Tony's."

Brin stood slightly shorter than Corey and blazed a look into her with the most beautiful green eyes Corey had ever seen. Too bad the look was one of contempt.

"We got it."

"I don't feel right leaving you here with the little one. Not when Tony's is just down the road a ways."

"Tony's is what? A garage?"

"Only one in town."

"I see."

"And how far is it?"

"About a five-minute drive up the road."

She seemed to think a moment and then nodded. "Okay. If you're sure you don't mind?"

Corey smiled, trying her best to be friendly. "I don't mind."

Brin closed the hood and then opened the back door and got Laken from her seat. Then they all crawled into the truck with Laken sitting in the middle. She at once became fascinated with the lap belt.

"Honestly, we could probably just walk," Brin said, rubbing her hands on her jeans.

"Glad to help," Corey said. "Like I said, it's no trouble."

"I can't believe the heat did it to the car," Brin said. She glanced over at her as the breeze blew her thick, blond hair. "But I guess I shouldn't be surprised. It damages everything else."

"Yeah, the heat will do it all right."

"Are you from Phoenix? Or have you lived here all your life?"

Corey was surprised at the personal question. "I'm from the Midwest originally. But I've lived here for the past thirty years or so."

"Oh. Wow."

"Wow, as in I'm old?" She chuckled.

"No," Brin said. "No, of course not. I didn't mean—"

"I'm teasing," Corey said. She winked at her and she could've sworn that Brin blushed before she looked away.

Corey wondered what the blush meant, if anything at all.

Laken played with the lap belt and then reached out and started messing with the radio knobs. She nearly blew out the speakers.

"Laken, no!" Brin grabbed her hand and adjusted the volume. "Sorry."

"It's all right," Corey said, chuckling again.

"She doesn't know any better."

"It's not a problem."

Brin sighed. "She just, she likes round things. Things that spin."

"And pumpkins," Corey added.

Brin looked at her. Then she smiled. "Yes, and pumpkins."

They pulled up to Tony's and Corey honked the horn to get his attention.

"He'll take good care of you."

"I can't thank you enough," Brin said, hand on the door handle.

"No need." Corey tugged on her cap. "You two take good care."

"Thanks, we will."

She opened the door after releasing Laken's lap belt. Then she slid from the car and held her arms out for Laken.

But Laken turned to Corey and looked up at her. Corey started to speak, but Laken surprised her by reaching up and taking her hat. She placed it promptly on her own head and tugged on the bill as if mimicking Corey.

Corey let out a boisterous laugh.

Brin seemed to be at a loss for words.

"She's never done that before."

"You like that?" Corey asked her. Laken crawled from the car without answering. Brin tried to remove the hat, but Laken cried out and secured it on her head.

"Laken, that's not yours," Brin said, obviously embarrassed. "I'm so sorry."

"You know what? Don't worry about it. Let her keep it."

Brin tried again to remove it, but Laken wouldn't have it.

"Brin," Corey said.

Brin glanced up at her as if she were surprised to hear her name.

"Seriously, let her keep it."

"Are you sure?"

Corey smiled. "Absolutely."

Brin finally nodded and closed the door. "Okay then. Thank you."

Corey nodded. "You're welcome." She put the truck in reverse as Tony came out to greet them.

Then she drove home, smile still stuck on her face, thinking about little Laken in her hat.

Chapter Four

Brin pulled up at the large house and eased into a rare parking space. Around her, people were climbing from their cars and heading toward the massive front door, most of them with children sprinting ahead, their excitement more than obvious. Brin, however, sat with a lump in her throat, anxious about going inside.

The two-story mansion belonged to Miley Roberts, a woman Brin had only just met a few days before. She'd been in town shopping and Miley had approached her at the market, introducing herself and insisting she come to her fall fiesta. It was going to be the party of the year, she'd said. Next to her New Year's celebration, that is. Brin had hardly even blinked before Miley had bounced with her hands in hers, answering for her. She'd said, "Great, see you then!" And off she'd gone, tousling Laken's hair as she left them. Laken had shied away from her and given a scowl, but Miley didn't seem to notice. Or care. Brin was betting on the latter.

It was then that Brin had allowed Laken to put Corey's hat back on her head. It had been the only thing to console her. And she'd worn the darn thing twenty-four-hours straight every day since. She even fell asleep with it on, leaving Brin to have to sneak in and remove it in the middle of the night. She'd washed it for her, along with Charlie the whale, and Laken had noticed but she didn't protest very much. She just seemed glad to wake up with them in her bed.

Now they were at Miley's party, and Laken was still insisting on wearing the hat. Brin allowed it, knowing it would be the only way to get her to go. They were already running late as it was and some battles just weren't worth it.

Brin eyed Laken in the rearview mirror. "You ready for the party, Lake? Should be fun."

Laken looked around but said nothing, the hat nearly swallowing her head. Brin opened the door and got her out and they headed inside, already able to hear pop music and smell smoky barbecue. They didn't bother knocking on the door, as no one else was, and Brin led Laken inside by the hand. The house was grand and beautiful with a large foyer and fancy staircase. Everything seemed to be decorated in black and white, even the floor. Brin had never seen anything like it, and she tried very hard not to stare with her mouth agape.

"Brin!" Brin turned and found Miley rushing up to her. "So glad you could come! And little Larkin too." Again, she rubbed Laken's head, causing Laken to shy away and scowl. "Isn't she just the cutest?" She smiled at Laken and then focused on her hat. "Is that one of Corey Durand's hats?"

Brin blushed despite herself. "Yes. Laken liked it so Corey gave it to her."

"Well, isn't that nice?" But Miley didn't sound pleased. She looked at Brin. "I take it you've met Corey then?"

"My neighbor? Yes, I have."

"Oh, that's right," she said, her overly made-up eyes narrowing. "You two are neighbors. How about that?" A strange look came over her then and Brin couldn't help but notice.

"What? What is it?"

"Oh, it's nothing." But she seemed to change her mind. "It's just that. Well, Corey's sort of like an old spinster. Only not your typical spinster." She leaned toward her as if she were about to share a secret. "She's a *lesbian.*"

Brin swallowed, almost too shocked to be offended. "Oh."

"Yes, and she hasn't, rumor has it, had a woman in a long while. So, I'd watch my back if I were you."

"I'm not too worried about it. Besides, I thought Corey was taken."

Miley's eyes widened like Brin had just spilled some major beans. "We need to talk, you and I."

Brin opened her mouth to tell her just what she thought of her rumors and opinions, and that the thought of gossiping with her made her nauseous, but Miley didn't give her time. She just smiled broadly and spoke. "She's here somewhere. Probably sulking in the corner. She isn't much for social occasions either."

"I wonder why she came then?" Brin asked, more than curious. Mainly because she was suddenly wishing that she hadn't. She didn't like Miley's tone or implications. Not one little bit, and she wondered if Corey was aware of how Miley really felt about her.

"Why for the pumpkins of course!" Miley said, motioning around. "She provided all the décor from her patch and she's here to plug it, hoping people will come to her farm for more."

"Oh, well, that sounds like a great idea," Brin said. Maybe Corey had no idea how Miley felt about her. How sad. Corey was probably there, innocently trying to promote her pumpkin patch, while this woman secretly berated her.

Brin felt sick.

Miley grinned, oblivious. "Brilliant, right? It was my idea."

"But you just said—"

"It was the only way I could get Corey to agree to provide the pumpkins for the party."

Brin blinked, unsure what to say. Miley was seriously rubbing her the wrong way.

Miley squeezed her upper arm and squealed. "Oh, here's the one I've been looking for." She waved over a tall man with mousy brown hair and bright blue eyes. Brin could at once see the resemblance along the eyes and mouth, but Miley put it to fact anyway. "Brin, this is my brother, Jimmy. Jimmy, this is Brin. The new gal in town I was telling you about." She winked. "I told you she was pretty."

Jimmy, who seemed to be just as comfortable with himself as his sister was with herself, grinned and took Brin's hand in both of his.

"Well, hello, angel. Where have you been all my life?"

Brin wanted to throw up in her mouth but managed to hold back. Instead, she slid her hand out from between his and rested it on Laken's shoulder.

"This is my niece, Laken."

"Oh, is it Laken, or Larkin?" Miley asked, hand to her chest.

"Laken."

"Anyway, Jimmy here owns the local used auto lot. Jimmy's Deals. He's very successful."

Brin politely smiled, feeling even more sick. "That sounds nice."

"I don't mean to brag, but I do very well. Especially for a town this size." He sank a hand in his pressed chinos and smoothed down the front of his button-down shirt. The shine on his loafers was nearly enough to cause Brin to squint. And his cologne… Brin fought backing away to lessen its effect.

"He's in business with the largest auto dealer in Flagstaff," Miley said, apparently more than proud.

Brin nodded. They were both obviously impressed with his stature, but she couldn't care less. She'd never date someone like

Jimmy, thanks to his being the wrong sex, much less befriend him. But the two seemed clueless and worse…hopeful. As if he actually stood a chance.

"Well, you two enjoy yourselves," Miley said, grinning from ear to ear. "Food's out back, along with the inflatable slide and ball pit. Have fun, Larkin," she said before she breezed off.

Brin clenched her jaw and pulled Laken close.

"My sister," Jimmy said with a laugh. "Tends to brag a bit about me. Just ignore her."

Brin tried to think of something to say, searched for a way out, but she found none. Jimmy was blocking the exit to the backyard.

Laken, who had allowed her to hold her tight for only a moment, began to squirm. Soon she'd pushed away and darted outside to a table where two small pumpkins sat. She immediately grabbed them and hurried farther away.

"Laken!" Brin left Jimmy talking and chased after her into the backyard. She slammed to a stop when she saw Laken standing with someone.

Corey Durand.

She'd never been so happy to see someone in her life.

"Laken!" Brin said breathlessly as she approached. Corey was kneeling in front of her, and she straightened when she saw Brin.

"Hi," she said with a polite smile.

"Hi." Brin felt herself flush again, but this time it was at Corey's appearance. She was wearing dark jeans and a crisp, white V-neck tee. Her short salt-and-pepper hair looked to be styled with product, and she smelled like heaven itself with a cologne that was fresh and clean-smelling and not nearly as overbearing as Jimmy's. It made Brin's mouth water.

"She's still fond of the hat," Corey said, slipping her hands into her back pockets.

"She refuses to take it off. Even sleeps with it."

"Really?" Corey laughed. "I see she's found some more pumpkins as well."

"Yes." Brin looked back toward the house. Jimmy was leaning against the doorjamb watching them. "Thank God she did. Otherwise I'd still be trapped inside with Jimmy Roberts."

Corey laughed. "Good ol' Jimmy. He knows how to charm the ladies."

"He literally made my skin crawl."

"He seems to have that effect on people. Women especially."

"I think Miley was trying to set us up."

"Oh, I don't doubt it."

Brin refocused on Laken and she knelt and tried to take the pumpkins away. Laken protested. Then Brin felt a gentle hand on her shoulder.

"She's okay," Corey said. "She's not hurting anything by carrying those around."

Brin stood, a little unnerved at being told what to do in regard to Laken.

"They're here for decoration, and I can't just let her do whatever she wants all the time."

"Maybe not. But right now, she's not bothering anyone, and she seems to be enjoying herself. Besides, it's great advertisement for my pumpkins."

Brin wanted to argue, but found she had no ground to stand on. Once again, Corey Durand had defused the situation.

God, how can someone be so calm and reasonable all the time? Or better yet, why can't I?

"Maybe you're right. Trying to get her to give up anything is damn near impossible without a serious meltdown."

"Sounds like you've been through quite a few."

"You have no idea."

Laken took off just then, and Brin and Corey followed her over to the ball pit. She stared inside for a while before she placed her pumpkins on the ground and then reached in for two balls. She held one in each hand and began walking around with them.

"Guess the pumpkins are old news," Corey said.

Brin smiled, unable not to. "I guess so."

They watched her for a long moment, weaving in and out of the other kids, virtually ignoring them before Corey spoke again.

"Is she—you know—"

"Autistic?"

Corey nodded.

"That's what they're telling me."

"They being who? Doctors?"

"Yes. But…"

"But?"

Brin looked at her and found the kindest, most understanding eyes she'd seen in a long, long while. For a moment, she was almost at a loss for words. "They want to put her on medication. Send her to a special school."

"Oh."

"And I'm not ready for that. My sister wasn't ready for that."

"Your sister?"

"Laken's my niece."

"Oh, I didn't realize."

"You mean Miley didn't tell you? I figured the whole town would know by now."

Corey laughed. "Somehow I missed the gossip where you're concerned."

She seemed almost disappointed, which surprised Brin. What was it she was wanting to know?

"My sister, Breana, passed away from breast cancer nine months ago. So, I took over care of Laken."

"I'm very sorry for your loss. That must've been hard."

"Thanks, it has been."

"That's very noble of you taking over care of your niece."

"I wouldn't have it any other way. And frankly, neither would Laken. She's not too keen on strangers, though you seem to be an exception."

Corey looked down at her feet as if she were embarrassed. "Yeah, well, I think I understand her a little. I'm not too keen on strangers either."

"Present company excluded?" Brin teased her.

What am I doing? Am I flirting?

Corey smiled. "Present company excluded."

I have to stop this. Now.

"So, where's your partner?"

Corey's eyebrows shot up. "Sorry?"

But just then, a woman screamed. Brin focused behind Corey and saw Laken pushing over a baby stroller. The stroller knocked into a nearby table, spilling the drinks. Laken was oblivious to the mess though, concentrating instead on spinning the wheels of the stroller once it was down on its side.

"Oh, my God," Brin said as she scrambled over to her, uprighting the stroller as quickly as she could.

The woman, the one who'd screamed, was hysterical. "My child could've been in there!"

"I'm so sorry," Brin said, taking Laken by the hand.

"Get control of yours," the woman fumed.

"Easy now," Corey said, coming up to stand beside Brin. "Laken didn't mean any harm."

The woman huffed and stormed away. Brin held onto Laken and tried to sop up the mess on the table. It was a difficult task with one hand.

"Here, let me," Corey said as she carefully took the paper towel from Brin.

"No, I've got it," Brin said, snapping at her. "It's Laken's mess and I should clean it up."

"You don't have to do it alone," Corey said, trying again.

"I do!" Brin let out. She slammed down the wet paper towel. "Don't you get it? I do have to do it alone!"

"Brin, I—"

"Just stop! You can't help me. No one can." She choked up and left the table, walking with Laken back toward the house. The crowd parted as they made their way, voices hushed and eyes trained on them.

Didn't anyone understand? She had to do things alone. She and she alone was responsible for Laken. She had to get used to caring for her, for solving whatever problem might arise. She couldn't depend on anyone else to do it for her.

Brin swallowed back tears, and just before she reached the front door, she removed Corey's hat and tossed it onto a table. Laken cried and Brin scooped her up kicking and screaming and headed for her car. Once inside, she strapped her in and started the vehicle up and sat there and cried. Only when she saw Corey emerge with her hat in her hand did she put the car in reverse and head home, crying the entire way.

CHAPTER FIVE

I don't get it," Grey said. "I thought you said everything was fine between you two. Good, even." She groaned as she straightened, carrying a large pumpkin. She ambled over to the trailer with it and set it down.

Corey knelt in the patch and cut her own large pumpkin free, then followed Grey to the trailer and set it down. Whip was right on her heels as they continued to gather pumpkins to move to the front of the ranch for decoration, to lure people in alongside the sign she'd just had erected. It was mindless work, leaving Corey plenty of free rein to discuss what had been on her mind for the last two days.

"That's what I thought," Corey said, recalling Miley's party. "But then she lost it when Laken knocked over some drinks. She wouldn't even let me help her clean up. She said she had to do it alone and that no one could help her."

Grey maneuvered her mouthful of sunflower seeds with her jaw. "Sounds like she's stressed out more than anything, and that that little girl is a handful."

Corey rubbed the back of her neck. "Yeah, she seems to be. But it's not her fault. She's…" Corey removed her ball cap and scratched her head.

"You ain't got to tell me," Grey said. "I already noticed it."

"What do you know about it?"

Grey eyed her. "Remember Randy, Maggie's little second cousin?"

"Oh, right."

"She was on the spectrum too."

Corey walked to another pumpkin, cut it free from the vine, and lifted it. "Brin seems to think Laken is as well. Though she's not happy about it. Says the doctors want to medicate her and all. Sounds like she's fighting doing so."

"Might be the best thing for her," Grey said. "You never know."

Corey set down the pumpkin and wiped her brow. Whip lay down and began tending to his paws. "Yeah, well, I get the sense that there may be more to the story. I'm thinking about referring her over to Tara."

"Tara?" She spit out some empty shells.

"It might be a good idea."

"I thought Tara worked in sensory and stuff like that?"

"She does. And that may be just what little Laken needs. At the very least Tara can evaluate her and give her her opinion. Tara's got a good eye for these kids and seems to know what it is they need."

"Too bad she wasn't better toward you after the breakup with Dawn."

"That's ancient history."

"Is it? I guess it must be if you're going to refer someone to her."

"She can help. And that's all that matters."

"You better hope she don't help too much. You know how she is."

"I trust she'll be professional."

"Uh-huh. If I remember correctly, she even made a pass at you some years back. When you was with Dawn."

"That was nothing. A fluke. She was a little drunk is all." Corey knelt next to another pumpkin and paused. "What makes you think she'd do the same to Brin?"

"Because Brin's an attractive woman, ain't she? And Tara's still breathing."

Corey waved her off. "Brin wouldn't fall for that. Besides, I don't even think she's into women."

"Ha. Right."

Corey glanced up at her. "What?"

"Your gaydar. It's seriously damaged."

"Why do you say that?"

"You kidding? I saw the way that woman was looking at you that very first day. Her trying to manage her hair, looking you up and down. She's interested."

Corey laughed. "Oh, good God, she is not."

"She was sizing you up like you was a main course."

"You're crazy, old woman."

"Like a fox."

Corey freed another pumpkin and brought it over to the trailer. Then she returned to the patch, cut free two small ones, and brought them back as well.

Grey was still resting by the trailer.

"You gonna help me, or just stand there?" she said to Grey.

"I'm liking standing here pretty good."

"Lazy old coot."

"We got enough already. You do any more and there won't be none left in the patch."

Corey counted ten good-sized pumpkins and agreed with Grey. They both climbed onto the four-wheel-drive Mule, along with Whip, and pulled the trailer back through the patch to the front of the ranch where they began to unload. They worked in silence for a while before Grey spoke up.

"Got you thinking about Dawn, didn't I?"

Corey squinted over at her. "Nah."

"You got awful quiet."

"Doesn't mean I'm thinking about her." There was a woman on her mind, but it wasn't her ex. And truth be told, she hadn't thought about Dawn in a long while and that felt good. She'd finally cut the last of the ties and she no longer worried about her or her well-being either. She just couldn't and it didn't matter what anyone had to say about it. Not anymore.

"You get quiet, it means you're thinking. So, I naturally assumed you was thinking about Dawn." She set down a pumpkin and turned her head to spit out some shells. "You heard from her lately?"

There for a while Dawn would call and want to talk. But Corey had quickly learned that almost every conversation led to her asking for money, so she'd stopped taking the calls. It hurt to admit it, but Dawn only seemed to care about one thing and one thing only. Herself.

"No. And I like it that way."

"Yeah, she finally stopped bugging me and Maggie too."

Corey cringed, hating that Dawn had even tried to get money out of her good friends. It made her sick just thinking about it.

"I'm sorry about that, Grey. She had no right to bother you two."

"Hell, it ain't your fault, Corey. It's just who she is."

"No, it's who she became. The goddamn pills did it to her."

Grey nodded and adjusted her cowboy hat. "I suppose you're right."

"Who she is now is not the woman I fell in love with."

They finished unloading the pumpkins and returned the trailer to the barn. Grey let the silence ensue this time and Corey was grateful. She took the Mule and called for Whip and they left Grey to tend to the pygmy goats.

The day was bright and sunny with a crisp breeze, and Corey wasn't even sure if what she was about to do was wise. But for whatever reason, it was in her to do it, and she wasn't about to back out now. She told herself it was because of Laken, but deep down she knew she wanted to see Brin just as badly as well.

She drove back through the patch and through the overgrown field to Brin's house with Whip sitting at her side. She hadn't been close to the house in years, and she was surprised to see that it still needed a lot of repairs. She would've thought that Brin would've had those fixed before she moved in. Yet here the house stood, with at least four major repairs needed that she could see.

She brought the Mule to the front and parked next to Brin's car. She was glad to see that Tony had helped her out, and she wondered if it had been the battery after all. She wasn't about to ask though. No, she needed this visit to go well.

She grabbed the two little pumpkins she'd picked and walked up the overgrown footpath to the front door. Whip followed and took his cue by resting near the front steps. He was used to waiting for her outside of folks' homes if they were unsure whether or not he was welcome. The porch squeaked loudly and she almost wondered if she even needed to ring the doorbell.

The door swung open as if to answer her question.

"Hi," Brin greeted her, though the look on her face was less than welcoming.

Nevertheless, Corey offered a big smile. "Hi." She held up the pumpkins. "I come in peace."

"Very funny." But she gave her a hint of a smile and glanced over her shoulder at Whip.

Corey lowered the pumpkins. "Come on, you and I both know she'll love them."

"That's what I'm afraid of."

Corey cocked an eyebrow.

"If she likes them she'll keep trying to run away to your patch to pick more."

"Ah."

"So, you see my hesitation in giving those to her."

"Well, how about this then? I keep her in pumpkins for as long as I can, and that way, she won't have the urge to come over to the patch?"

"Until the pumpkin season is over. Then what?"

Corey shrugged. "Little balls?"

Brin laughed a little. "And you're willing to keep her in those?"

"If I have to."

Brin crossed her arms over her chest and Corey noticed the paint stains on her long-sleeved tee. Her sweats were also stained.

"Did I interrupt something?"

"I was just doing some painting." She hitched her thumb back inside the house. "The living room…" She motioned for her to come inside. "Why don't I just show you?"

Corey followed her in and saw stacks of boxes in the family room and a half-painted wall in the living room.

Brin remained at the door. "What about your dog?"

"Whip? He'll be fine out there."

Brin closed the door and Corey focused on Laken who was sitting on the covered floor coloring in a big coloring book.

"Hey, Laken," Corey said. But the girl didn't look up.

"She's playing Picasso, so she'll be at it for hours."

Corey studied her coloring. It was impressive. "She's really good."

"You should see her draw."

"I'd love to."

Brin studied her for a moment as if to see if what she'd said was the truth, then glanced around. "Please excuse the mess. The house is a fixer-upper and I'm only one person, so it's going to be a mess for a while."

"Do you need any help?" Corey asked, looking around. She spotted a million things she could do that would probably be a big help.

"No, we're good."

Corey thought about arguing but decided against it. After the fiasco at the party she didn't think it wise.

"Well, you know where to find me should you change your mind."

Brin nodded and Corey got the feeling her time was near up.

"I bet you're wondering why I came by."

"It had crossed my mind."

Corey reached in her back pocket and pulled out her wallet. Then she plucked out a business card and handed it over.

"This is my friend Tara. She runs a place called the Sensory Path in Flagstaff and—"

"And you think I should take Laken there?" The pinched look on her face spoke volumes, and Corey knew she'd crossed a line she shouldn't have.

"Well, I—yes. It's not like other places—"

"Look, I don't need you or anyone else telling me how to take care of my niece, okay?" She flung the card back toward Corey and it fell to the floor. "I'll do what I think is best for her."

"I'm not trying to tell you what to do. I—"

"No? Are you sure about that? After what happened at the party and everything? Because it seems to me you showed up here to do just that. Well, I don't need any help. Not with the house, and especially not with Laken."

"Brin, let me explain."

But Brin had uncrossed her arms and moved to the front door. She held it open and motioned for Corey to walk through.

"I don't need you to. I've heard it all before, trust me. And you can tell Miley I said the same. The last thing I need is for that woman to show up on my doorstep again."

"Miley came by?" Corey asked as she hurried outside.

"As if you didn't know."

"I swear I didn't. What did she say? Brin, listen, I have nothing to do with Miley Roberts. I—"

Brin scoffed. "Yeah, whatever."

"No, I swear." Damn Miley. What had she said?

"Uh-huh. Good-bye, Corey."

She closed the door and bolted it, leaving Corey standing all alone on the front porch. Corey stood very still, unsure if she should even move. Eventually, she placed the little pumpkins on a nearby rocking chair and then lifted her hat off her head and set it down next to them. Then, with one last look at the house, she mouthed an apology and crawled into her Mule and drove away with Whip, all the while wondering just what in the hell she'd done that was so wrong.

CHAPTER SIX

The words on the laptop began to blur and Brin blinked, trying to stave off the nap that was insistent on coming. She tried to focus, but soon the words blurred again and she knew it was no use. Concentrating had been difficult and not just because of fatigue. She'd gone over and over her last encounter with Corey and she couldn't help but be confused. Had Corey really spoken the truth when she'd said she had nothing to do with Miley Roberts? Or was she playing coy, trying, like she suspected Miley of doing, to get her foot in the door with her just so she could judge her and spread more gossip? She'd like to think that Corey was telling the truth, but the way Miley had acted when she'd shown up uninvited after the party had her doubting everyone. According to Miley, Laken had caused quite the circus and she'd insisted that Brin get her into intensive behavioral therapy and put her on medication. She hadn't wanted to hear Miley's explanation about her being suspected of being on the spectrum. All she'd seemed to care about was the fact that Laken had caused a ruckus at her party. And according to her, it seemed everyone else who was there felt the same. That included Corey.

She rubbed her eyes and looked to the clock. She'd been working for two hours now. Time for a break from work and a break from wondering about Corey Durand and her intentions.

She stood and stretched and headed for the bathroom. When she finished there, she headed for Laken's room, expecting to wake her from her afternoon nap. But to her horror, she found that Laken was not in bed. And Charlie, the whale, was on the floor.

"Oh, no. Laken!" Brin tore through the house in a panic, shouting her name. But in room after room, she came up empty. And when she finally reached the back door, she found it open and the entryway barren. She rushed outside and searched for Laken in the pumpkin patch. She couldn't see her.

"Oh, Jesus, God, no." Brin slipped on her shoes, grabbed her car keys, and raced to her car. She started it up and peeled out, speeding around the road to Corey's ranch. When she reached the front, she saw a sign for the pumpkin patch and she sped past it. She pulled around the house and screeched to a stop outside of a big barn where she saw Corey kneeling next to Laken, feeding little goats.

Brin took a moment to thank whatever higher being there was in the universe and then scrambled from the car and slammed the door. She stalked over to Corey and Laken so mad she could hardly breathe.

"How dare you keep her without letting me know where she is," she seethed.

Corey didn't bother to look over at her. Neither did Laken, but that wasn't a surprise.

"I would have, if I'd had your number," she eventually said, just as calm as a cucumber.

"You should've brought her home. Right away."

Corey kept talking softly to Laken as they fed the goats.

"Damn it, listen to me!" Brin said.

Corey finally straightened. But not before she poured the food from her hand into Laken's little ones. The two goats fought over themselves to get to the food. Laken giggled.

"She hasn't been here long," Corey said. "Maybe ten minutes. I found her wandering through the patch and figured you'd come for her soon enough."

"You figured I'd come for her soon enough? Are you kidding me? I was worried sick!"

"Well, then, we should probably exchange phone numbers, don't you think? Since this is bound to be a regular occurrence."

"It's not going to be a regular occurrence," Brin said, stomping past her. "And I don't like what you're insinuating."

"Look, this isn't my idea of a good time either. A small child having the run of my ranch worries me. Worries me a lot."

"Well, then I'll make damn sure she doesn't ever set foot here again."

"How are you gonna do that?" She chuckled and it infuriated Brin.

"Don't worry. I'll figure it out."

Brin took Laken by the hand and tugged her along after her. Laken cried and dragged her feet. Brin scooped her up and carried her to the car.

"It's okay," she said, trying to soothe her. "We'll play games when we get home. Let's just please get home."

And away from Corey Durand.

But Laken wouldn't have it. She kept crying and kicking and shaking her head.

"Here," Corey said, coming up from behind. She pulled off her hat and placed it on Laken's head. Laken stopped crying instantly and fingered the brim.

"There," Corey said. "That's better."

"Great. Now I have to break her from that again."

"It's better than her screaming," Corey said softly.

Brin put Laken in her car seat and buckled her up. To her dismay, she found that Corey was right. The hat had calmed her. She was busy playing with it, lifting it on and off her head.

"I don't need any help," Brin said.

"Right. I forgot."

"Don't get sarcastic with me," Brin said, opening her own door.

"Look," Corey said, holding up her hands. "I'm not trying to piss you off or step on your toes or whatever else it is you think I'm trying to do. I only want peace."

"Then maybe you should stay out of our way." Brin regretted it the second she said it, but she was so angry she was nearly out of control. Angry that Laken once again escaped without her having a clue, angry that she ran to Corey, and angry that Corey had such a good way with her. Why did it have to be Corey of all people that Laken had to take to?

Corey dropped her hands, a look of defeat on her face. "I'm sorry, I guess we're not going to get anywhere, are we?"

Brin softened and almost teared up. "No, I'm sorry," she said, shaking her head. "I'm just so damn overwhelmed. I'm doing the best I can, but it doesn't seem to be good enough. This time she got out while I thought she was sleeping. The house was quiet, I was working, and she got out without making a sound."

Corey looked concerned. "How did she get out?"

"The back door. I had it locked, but apparently she knows how to turn the lock."

"I think I can help," Corey said. "If you'll let me?"

Brin studied her and tried to size her up. Was this another ploy to try to stick her nose in where it didn't belong, like Miley? Or was she genuinely concerned and wanting to help? Brin thought about how good to them she'd been thus far. But then she remembered how she needed to do this on her own. She couldn't depend on anyone else. It wasn't in her and Laken's best interest to do so.

Corey seemed to read her mind. "Or, how about I show you what to do and you do it?"

Brin smiled a little. "Am I that obvious?"

"You're pretty obvious."

She palmed her forehead. "God, I'm sorry. I'm just at my wits' end and I'm really trying to do everything myself."

"I understand," Corey said. "Which is why I'll just show you what to do. Why don't you give me a half an hour and then I'll meet you at your house?"

Brin raised an eyebrow.

"Trust me," Corey said. "Can you do that?"

"I can try."

Corey smiled. "Good."

❖

Corey knocked on the door exactly half an hour later and held up a small plastic bag and a cordless drill. Brin let her in and tried not to stare at her taut backside as she walked toward the back door. The smell of hay and sweat coming off her did nothing to detour Brin's libido. In fact, it only seemed to heighten it.

Get control, Brin. Focus.

She realized that Corey's attractiveness was definitely another reason why she wanted so desperately to keep her away. It seemed every time she saw her, her skin warmed and tingled and her heart did a little dance in her chest.

Corey set the bag on the table, and for a second, she seemed to catch Brin staring.

"Something wrong?" she asked as she pulled out her goods.

"Hm? No, nothing."

"I know I'm dirty. But it kinda comes with the gig."

"I'm not thinking anything bad."

"No?"

"No."

"What were you thinking, then?"

Brin blushed and looked away. *God, if you only knew.* "So, what did you get?"

"Safeguards. For the doors."

"Oh." Brin felt ridiculous. "Guess I should've thought of that."

"Yeah, well, you didn't know she could unlock the doors."

"No, I didn't. Even so, I should've thought of it."

"These," Corey said, holding one up. "You place them up high, where she can't reach them. Then you flip it over when you're inside the house and she won't be able to open the doors."

"Okay. Great."

"If you want, you can help me by holding this in place while I screw it in. That way you can see how to do it."

Brin knew how to use a drill. She could easily screw the safeguards into place herself, but something in her made her agree. That something, she knew, was the ever-growing powerful desire to be near Corey. Yet, she couldn't fight it. And at the moment, she didn't want to.

"Of course." Brin cleared her throat and stood next to her. She held the piece in place while Corey drilled in the screws. She tried not to stare at her angular face, her salt-and-pepper temples, or her steel blue eyes. But damn it, it was difficult not to with their close proximity, and soon Brin was trying to control her breathing, her desire nearly taking complete control. She was so frazzled that she lost her grip on the safeguard causing Corey to lose a screw. They both knelt to retrieve them and bumped heads.

Brin stumbled backward, gripping her forehead. "I'm so sorry."

Corey had her hat in her hand, rubbing the top of her head. "No worries." She held up the screw. "I got it." She replaced her hat and then motioned for Brin to hold the safeguard once again. Brin did, though with slightly trembling hands, and they finished fastening it into place.

"You want to try the next one?"

Brin nodded, though she really had no desire to work the drill. She was happy to let Corey continue to do it. There was just something about her working that drill that was doing something for her. Maybe it was the way her sinewy forearms moved, or the way she clenched her strong jaw as she worked. Whatever it was, it was doing it for her and she didn't care that she was quickly approaching the fine line of showing her admiration. She just wanted to keep staring at her.

Somehow they finished with the back door without her drooling all over herself and they headed for the front, where Corey opened the package and held the guard in place. She waited patiently as Brin readied the drill. But Brin's hand was still shaky, and when she tried to drill in the screw it fell. They almost bumped heads again, but Corey beat her to it and held up the screw.

"Here you go." She handed it over and then placed her hand over Brin's to secure the drill. "Try to hold it steady and strong, like this."

Brin's heart rate tripled. "Steady and strong."

"Uh-huh."

Kind of like you.

She tried to control her breathing again but it was no use. She was full-on having a heated experience with her new, probably very involved, neighbor. But then Miley's words replayed in her mind. The ones about Corey not having a woman for a very long time. Could it be true? Could Corey be single? And available? And...interested?

Brin screwed the guard into place and then backed away, feigning a cough.

Corey didn't seem to notice. "That should do it."

"Yes, thank you."

"You're welcome."

She gathered her drill and stood by the front door. Laken ran to her and held up a small pumpkin, one of the ones Corey had given her.

"Why thank you, Laken."

Laken took off back down the hallway, Corey's hat still on her head.

"Would you like your hat back?" Brin asked. Then she remembered she still had the one Corey had left for Laken earlier. "Wait here a sec." She grabbed it off the top of the fridge and handed it to her. "This is the one you left the other day."

"Ah." Corey took it and let it rest against her thigh.

Brin stood awkwardly, twisting her hands. "Thanks again for your help."

"Sure." Corey began to dig in her back pocket and Brin panicked, worried she was going to retrieve another business card for her friend who ran the sensory place in Flagstaff. Her skin flushed with emotion as Corey did indeed pull out a business card, but she explained quickly. "My number, should you need it."

"Oh, right. Thanks."

Corey pulled out her cell phone and took Brin's number from her.

They stood awkwardly once again.

"Well, I should be off," Corey said. "A lot of work to be done before the pumpkin patch opens on Saturday."

"I can imagine," Brin said. "I'd offer to help, but with Laken—"

"No need," Corey said. "We've got it covered. But I do hope you'll stop by. We have more little pumpkins and some small squash that I think Laken will like."

"Thanks, I'll think about it."

Corey smiled. "Call if you need anything."

"Will do." She showed Corey out, watched her walk to her truck, and then collapsed against the door, heart still careening in her chest.

"What am I gonna do?"

Laken ran in the room with another small pumpkin and stopped dead in her tracks when she saw that Corey was gone. She burst into tears and ran away.

Brin nearly melted with defeat, the door suddenly not nearly strong enough.

"What am I gonna do?"

CHAPTER SEVEN

"My God, I think we may have actually bitten off more than we can chew," Corey said as she slowed the Mule to steer through a cluster of people. It was Saturday afternoon, the opening day of the pumpkin patch, and Corey was shocked at the throng of people that had turned out.

"Word spreads fast," Grey said from the seat next to her. "All these city folk coming up from Phoenix are excited to get themselves some pumpkins in some cooler weather."

"I guess so," Corey said.

"That and all the advertising in town seems to have helped a bunch."

"True. Remind me to thank everyone."

"You won't need reminding, but okay."

Corey rounded a kettle corn vendor and then parked beside one of the two face painters.

"Who knew we'd need all this to sell pumpkins?"

Grey chuckled. "People expect to be entertained these days. Or didn't you get the memo?"

"I guess I'm out of the loop."

"Yeah, well, Miley Roberts may be a lot of things, but she was right about you having all this. Without it, people would be bored."

"We have the goats and the baby chicks. And some of Mrs. Pettigrew's peach preserves for sale. Isn't that enough?"

"Boring," Grey said.

They sat and stared at the bouncy castle across from the barn. Kids were jumping and shrieking with joy. Corey couldn't help but smile.

"You check in with Ryan lately?" Corey asked.

Grey spit out some sunflower seed shells. "Yep. He's doing fine. Says sales are going well."

"Well, that's good, I suppose."

"Good? Hell, ain't this what you wanted?"

Corey took a long look around at all the people. She inhaled the scent of kettle corn and the cotton candy. Watched as a few kids fed the pygmy goats, laughing as the goats knocked the food from their hands. Then she watched as parents pulled wagons full of pumpkins toward the front, on their way to the cashier. All in all, it was a beautiful scene and she couldn't be more proud.

"You know, it is. It's exactly what I wanted."

"Good, cuz I was beginning to worry you'd lost your damn mind. Settin' all this up and then not being happy about it. I was about to smack you upside the head."

Corey laughed. "I'd like to see you try, old woman."

"I'd love to try."

Just then Ryan came on over the radio requesting backup at the checkout stand.

"I'll go," Grey said. "Seeing as how you've got company and all."

"Sorry?"

Grey elbowed her and nodded toward Brin and Laken who were headed right for them.

"Right."

Corey crawled from the Mule and Grey slid behind the wheel and took off toward the front of the ranch, leaving some dust in her wake.

"Hi," Brin said as she approached, holding Laken's hand.

"Hi." Corey knelt and got to Laken's eye level. "Hi, Laken." She was wearing Corey's hat and it nearly melted her heart. "I like your hat," she said, straightening once again.

Laken promptly removed the hat and extended it to her.

"Ah, thank you. But you keep it, okay? It looks good on you." She winked at her and Laken returned the hat to her head.

Brin seemed beside herself. "She only ever does that with you."

"What's that?"

"Interact."

"Oh." Corey shrugged. "Maybe she just likes me."

"Maybe," Brin said with a small smile. Her gaze traveled beyond Corey back toward the front of the ranch. Corey turned and saw her staring at Grey.

"I didn't mean to interrupt," Brin finally said. "With your partner and all."

"Who, Grey? Nah, she'll get over it."

Brin blinked at her. "She will?"

Corey laughed. "Of course. She had to go help out up front anyway."

Corey studied Brin as she studied her, looking back and forth from Grey to Corey.

"Wait," Corey said. "When you say partner, you don't mean…"

"As in," Brin said.

Corey burst out laughing. "Uh no, you got that all wrong."

"I do?"

Corey laughed so hard she could feel herself reddening. "Uh, yeah. Definitely. Grey's an old friend. And she's been married for years to a woman who would kick my ass if I even thought about hitting on her."

Brin appeared to be embarrassed. She shifted her feet and blushed. "Oh."

Corey shook her head. "You really thought…"

"I did."

"Oh, geez. Grey's gonna get a kick out of that."

"Glad I could be a little comic relief," she said with a smile.

Corey finally settled down and held out her hand for Laken. "Come on, let's go pick some squash."

Laken allowed her to take her hand and they walked over to the patch where there was a table set up with dozens of squash. Corey released her hand and pointed.

"Take your pick, kiddo."

Laken began playing with squash after squash. Corey retrieved a basket and gave it to Brin.

"You're spoiling her," Brin said with a chuckle.

"Hey, imagine if all kids only wanted squash. What a world it would be."

"You've got a good point."

Brin held the basket out and Corey grabbed the squash that Laken discarded and set them inside. She knew she couldn't decide, so she'd give her as many as she wanted to take home.

"I think that's enough," Brin said.

"Not yet," Corey said, watching Laken. Then, finally it happened. Laken settled on two squash that she didn't want to put down. "Bingo."

Brin shook her head. "How did you know?"

"I just pay attention." She took the basket from Brin and carried it for her as they continued to walk the ranch. "I knew she'd eventually find two she wanted to hold on to. And the others, she can keep to play with when she gets bored with those two."

"You're so good with her," Brin said. "My sister, she'd be so amazed."

They walked quietly for a few moments with Laken concentrating on her squash.

"You know, when we get home, she'll line all the squash up with her pumpkins."

"No kidding?"

"Yep. She loves to line things up. Entertains her for hours."

They came upon the pygmy goats and Laken began to shriek with excitement.

"Guess this means we're stopping here," Corey said. She led them into the fenced off area and set the basket in the barn. Then she scooped out a large handful of feed for Laken and called her over. Laken ran to her but seemed to struggle inwardly with what to do with her squash.

"Would you like me to hold them?" Corey asked.

Laken shifted a little and set the squash on the ground. Then she held out her hands for the feed. Corey gave her the food and the goats immediately hurried over and buried their faces in her hands. Laken giggled with delight and dumped the feed on the ground, already wanting more.

"Laken, you've already had some," Brin said.

"That's okay," Corey said. "Laken, can I lift you up?" Gently, she lifted Laken and set her up on a grated platform. Then she placed the bucket of feed next to her and showed her how to toss the food down to the goats. Laken at once went to the bucket and grabbed a handful of feed. But she didn't toss it down on the ground. Instead, she sat and dropped pieces of the food through the grates, watching as it fell down to the goats. She seemed mesmerized.

"Looks like she's entertained," Corey said, sitting down on the edge next to her. Brin eased down on the other side.

"It doesn't take much," she said. Brin once again smiled at her as she squinted into the sun and Corey noticed just what an incredibly attractive woman she was. With her blond hair and deep green eyes, she was a stunner. And then there was her body. Curved in all the right places and thick with muscle, it was no wonder her heart rate was starting to increase whenever she caught sight of her. But damned if she was going to tell anyone. Grey would give her all kinds of shit, and as for anyone else, they'd just bring up Dawn and that was something she wasn't willing to get into.

"Well, look who it is!"

Corey cringed as she recognized the shrillness of her voice.

"Hello, Miley."

Miley hurried up to them and reached for Laken's head, which she gave a good roughhousing. Laken balked and pushed her hand away.

"Oh, sorry, little one," Miley said, but she didn't sound sorry at all.

"She doesn't like touch a whole lot," Brin said, her voice sounding tight.

Corey recalled what Brin had said about Miley showing up at her house after the party, apparently saying things about Laken. It seemed she was still upset over the matter. Corey couldn't blame her. Miley seriously knew how to rub people the wrong way and butt in when she had no business doing so.

"No matter," Miley said, seemingly oblivious. "Let's talk about this shindig," she said, waving her well-manicured hands around. "Talk about a success!"

"It has turned out nicely," Corey said, wishing she would go away.

"Nicely? Come on, Corey, this is fabulous. You've got cars lined up to get in."

"I don't know about that." She knew Miley was exaggerating, but that seemed to come with the territory where she was concerned. "But it is going very well."

Miley grinned, showing off her stark white veneers. "And what about you?" she asked, referring to Brin. "You look like you're enjoying yourself. In fact, if I'm not mistaken, I'd say the three of you look like a little family sitting here feeding the goats." She looked down at her feet, as if making sure she wasn't stepping in goat poop.

"Oh, no," Brin said. "We're just letting Laken enjoy the goats." She gave what appeared to be a forced smile. Corey almost laughed at its obvious sarcasm, which seemed to be completely lost on Miley.

"With that hat on she looks like a little Corey Durand sitting there," Miley said. "Wouldn't that be a hoot, Corey?"

Corey flexed her jaw, growing frustrated. She didn't want Miley to scare Brin off.

Why couldn't she just go away? And why did she always have to run her mouth?

"Corey's great with Laken," Brin surprised her by saying. "And I think the matching hat is cute. Laken's really taken to her."

Miley's eyebrows shot up. "Really? Well, I see."

"There's nothing to see, Miley," Corey said, standing, already sensing where Miley might be heading. "Laken's just feeding the goats."

"Well, then I guess there's nothing wrong with Jimmy coming by to say hello to Brin then?"

Corey fought cringing again, but Miley didn't seem to notice or care. She looked to Brin.

"He saw you earlier and he's just dying to say hello."

Brin smiled again, so forced it looked like her cheeks would crumble.

"Jimmy's free to do what he wants," Brin said.

Miley bounced a little. "Very good. I'll send him over. Corey, congrats again on a big success. Hopefully, this little endeavor will line your pockets some." With that she turned and hurried away, watching the ground carefully as if she were once again worried about the goat poop.

Corey sighed, exasperated, and removed her hat to scratch her forehead.

"Is she always so…" Brin started.

"Offensive? Pushy? Nosy?" Corey laughed. "Not all the time. Sometimes she sleeps."

Brin cracked up. "Really? I was beginning to wonder about that too."

Corey slapped her hat against her thigh. "I gave up trying to figure that woman out years ago."

"I can understand why. It seems to be exhausting."

"Uh-huh."

"I just don't get it. One minute she's very nice and doing really nice things, and the next she's stabbing you with daggers right into your back."

"Sometimes into your front," Corey said, returning her hat to her head. "Sometimes she doesn't even try to hide her intentions or her dismay. She just flat out smacks you in the face with them."

"So, you're aware of some of the things she says about you?"

Corey scoffed. "Oh, yeah."

"And yet you still put up with her?"

"I'm not the only one she talks about. And what good would it do to shun her? She'd just talk more. No, I prefer to kill her with kindness. Besides, she's not all wrong. I am an old spinster." She winked.

Brin laughed.

"As well as a fanged lesbian predator. So you better look out."

"Oh, I'm terrified. Truly."

They both laughed and Brin cocked her head. "So you're not terribly fond of her either? I was worried you two were friends."

Corey smiled. "Just like Grey and I were partners?" She nudged her playfully.

Brin shoved her back just as playful. "Shut up."

"Your powers of perception are somewhat skewed a little don't you think?"

"No, they're not. You can't blame me for thinking that about you and Grey."

"Why? Because we're both obviously gay, so we must be together then?"

Brin stared at her. "I guess you got me there."

"Uh-huh."

"Hey, at least I admitted it."

"Yes, you did. And I forgive you. Most straight people make that assumption as well."

Brin blinked. "Straight? I'm not straight."

Corey's throat seized and she blinked back at her. "You… aren't?"

"Uh, no. Now who's making assumptions?"

Corey looked into her beautiful eyes, stunned. She knew she shouldn't be, especially with what Grey had said about her, but yet she was. Her heart raced and she found it difficult to swallow. She opened her mouth, unsure what to say, but knowing she needed to say something, anything.

But another voice beat her to it.

A voice that made her skin crawl.

CHAPTER EIGHT

So this is where all the good-looking women are hanging out," Jimmy Roberts said as he approached with a wide, sloppy grin. His gaze was fixed on Brin and she felt like squirming, like she was a helpless ant beneath the rays of the sun shining through a magnifying glass, Jimmy the devious child holding the glass.

"Why thank you, Jimmy," Corey surprised her by saying. She batted her eyelashes at him. "You do know how to make a lady swoon."

Jimmy glanced at her and grimaced, then returned his sights on Brin. "And how are you this fine day?"

"I'm…well, fine." She gave a pleasant smile but offered him nothing further. It seemed to disappoint him.

"Oh. Well, that's good. Nice to hear." He glanced at Corey nervously and then offered his elbow to Brin. "I thought you might want to take a walk around the grounds?"

Brin straightened. "That sounds like a great idea." She stood. "I would love a tour."

Jimmy smiled. "Fantastic."

But Brin ignored him and looked back to Corey and extended her own elbow toward her. "Care to show me around your place, Ms. Durand? I'd love to see it and who better to show me than you?"

Corey seemed to hesitate for a second, but then stood with a big smile. "I'd be honored."

They both grinned at Jimmy who seemed to be at a loss for words.

"It was nice seeing you, Jimmy," Brin said, hoping he would get the hint.

He stared at them for a moment or two and then stuttered. "I—I guess I'll see you around then." He walked away, his discontent more than obvious.

"See ya," Brin said.

Corey shook her head as they watched him exit the goat pen. "I didn't think you had it in you," she said.

Brin chuckled. "I don't like people forcing things on me. Especially when they aren't welcome."

"I'm beginning to see that."

Brin knelt and focused on Laken. "Lake, come on, hon, we're going to go for a walk with Corey."

Laken kept playing with the goats by dropping the feed down through the grates. She didn't look up once, and when her hands were empty she went back to the bucket almost as if in a trance.

"Laken," Brin said. "Come on, hon." She touched her hand and Laken pulled away.

"She's fixated," Corey said.

"Uh-huh." Brin straightened and sighed. "It's moments like these when I don't know what to do. If I make her quit she'll have a fit. If I wait for her to finish on her own, we'll be here all day."

Corey seemed to think a moment. Then she knelt and removed the bucket. She carried it into the barn and at first Laken didn't notice, too entranced to pay attention. But when her hands came up empty and she went for more feed, she seemed truly startled and she started to scream.

The children around them began scurrying and covering their ears. Brin quickly scooped her up and hurried her from the pen. Corey was right behind her, along with Whip.

"I don't know what to do," Brin said, panicked. Laken was screaming in her ear and kicking her feet.

"Over here," Corey said, leading them through the masses up to her home. She unlocked the back door and ushered Brin and Laken inside. Whip ran and jumped up on the large couch where Corey motioned for Brin and Laken to sit.

"Will she drink juice?" she asked from the adjoining kitchen.

"Only from a sippy cup." She set Laken down and dug in her purse. "Here." She held an empty one out for Corey.

Laken kept crying. Corey took the cup and filled it with juice. She returned quickly, cup in hand. "It's mango-pineapple. Hopefully, she'll like it."

"We'll see," Brin said, willing to try anything.

She gave the juice to Laken who tossed it on the floor.

"Laken," Brin said. "It's juice. You like juice."

Laken continued to cry. But to Brin's amazement, Whip moved closer to her and rested his chin in her lap, as if she were as calm as he was. Laken stopped crying and blinked down at the dog. Brin stroked his head.

"Good dog," she said softly.

Laken touched his head. Then, ever so carefully, she began to mimic Brin's movements and pet the dog. Whip wagged his tail and remained still.

"Animals," Corey said, picking up the sippy cup from the floor.

Brin looked at her, hoping she would explain.

"She likes animals."

"Mm." Brin looked back to Laken. "Seems so."

"First the goats, now the dog. They reach her somehow."

"How do we explain you?" Brin asked with a smile.

Corey sat on the ottoman and shrugged. "Maybe I'm animal-like."

Brin laughed and wiped away a tear.

"Hey," Corey said, touching her shoulder. "It's alright."

Brin shook her head. "It's not, but thanks."

Corey crossed back to the kitchen. "Mango-pineapple okay with you?"

"Sure."

Corey poured them both a glass and fumbled with the remote. "Does she like television?"

"Only if it's *Thomas the Tank Engine*."

Corey found a children's channel and thumbed up the volume a little.

"What about *Bubble Guppies*?"

"Guess that'll have to do."

Corey motioned for her to join her at the kitchen bar. Brin left Laken with Whip and sat next to Corey to sip her juice.

"Mm, God, that's good."

Corey grinned. "You're easy to please."

"What can I say, I'm a cheap date." She coughed a little as she realized what she'd implied. "Can't say my niece is easy to please though." They glanced back at her. She seemed to be watching television.

"Maybe she just has high standards," Corey said.

Brin sighed and took a moment to take in Corey's home. It was every bit the ranch home she'd imagined it to be with dark wood floors and cabinetry, large fireplace with a beautiful mantel, tasteful southwestern artwork, and oversized, comfortable-looking leather furniture. It felt welcoming and warm, and she felt safe there, which was odd, it being her first time inside the home.

Her eyes grew heavy as if they too felt comfortable enough to relax, and suddenly she longed to stretch out with Laken on the couch and take a nap while Corey looked on, tending to a roaring fire.

"You look tired," Corey said, bringing her back to the present.

"Me? Nah." She sipped her drink and her eyes teared. "Ha. Who am I kidding? I'm exhausted." She wiped away another tear and laughed. "What was I thinking, thinking I could do this all on my own?"

"No one can do everything totally on their own, Brin. Even the best of folks need help sometime."

Brin met her intense gaze and then refocused on her drink. "I have to do it on my own, Corey. It's just Laken and me. No one else. I can't depend on anyone else."

"That's bullshit," Corey let out. "Sorry."

Brin smiled.

"Seriously," Corey continued. "Asking and accepting help when you need it takes courage. There's absolutely nothing wrong with it. And who says you have to do everything alone just because you're on your own? Who came up with that crazy rule? I'm on my own and I have to have all kinds of help."

"Really?"

"Sure. Ryan and Grey and the rest of my farmhands. The whole town helped me advertise for today, not to mention the high school kids I hired on to help. All it took was a little asking."

"I don't know," Brin said. "I've always been taught to do things myself."

"There comes a time when it's okay to ask for help, Brin."

Brin nodded and took another sip of her drink. "I suppose you're going to encourage me to call your friend, aren't you?"

"Oh no, I've learned my lesson."

Brin laughed. "I scared you away?"

"Yes, ma'am."

"Really? That's all it took?"

"Uh-huh."

"Well, you're no fun."

"I'm no glutton for punishment either."

"Okay, okay. Just tell me she has nothing to do with Miley Roberts and I'll consider it."

"She has nothing to do with Miley Roberts."

"Sold."

Corey sipped her drink. She smiled.

Brin shifted, uneasy. "You wouldn't happen to have another one of her cards would you?"

"It just so happens." Corey dug into her back pocket and pulled out her wallet. She plucked out a card and handed it over. "Give her website a look before you call if you like. That way you can see firsthand why I thought it might be a good fit for you and Laken."

"She doesn't push medication?"

"She doesn't push anything."

Brin glanced at the card. "Okay. But no promises."

Corey held up her palms. "No promises."

They both stared at Laken on the couch. She was still and Corey got up and crept around the corner of the sofa to look.

"They're asleep."

Brin smiled. "I'm ready for a nap myself. I better get home."

"I'll drive you." Corey unfastened her radio and spoke into it, asking for the Mule to be brought to the front of the house.

"Thank you so much for everything," Brin said.

"You're welcome." Corey touched her arm. "And don't be afraid to ask for anything in the future."

Brin nodded and stared at her hand on her arm. Corey removed it and they glanced away from one another as if the moment had grown too heavy.

Brin moved from the stool as she heard the Mule arrive. "I better get Laken."

She scooped her up from the couch and Whip followed them to the door. Corey helped her get settled in the Mule and Whip jumped on the back seat. They drove in silence back to Brin's

"Thank you, again," Brin said

Corey smiled. "Have a nice evening."

"Thanks, you too." She turned and looked at Whip. "Thanks to you too, boy." He wagged his tail and Brin walked up the front porch with Laken asleep in her arms. As she walked inside her house, she turned and gave Corey one last, long look.

Now, why couldn't I have ever had someone like her in my life?

But as she closed the door, she closed the thought out with it.

It was time to focus on Laken once again.

Chapter Nine

"You gonna tell me what happened with your lady friend on Saturday or do I have to guess?" Grey asked as they walked through the patch, checking on more pumpkins.

Another good weekend like the one before and they'd be all but sold out. Halloween was coming up and she knew they'd be lucky to have enough pumpkins to last until then. She couldn't believe it, but the patch had been a big success so far. So much so that next year they'd have to go bigger and plant more.

"Like you could guess," Corey said, kneeling to turn one over for some sunlight. The day was crisp and overcast, not a good day for sunbathing pumpkins. But she hoped the weather forecast was wrong and that they'd see more sun than expected in the next few days.

Grey scoffed. "It ain't hard. She's growing on ya. Her and that kiddo both."

"No," Corey said, straightening. But she knew she sounded defensive and she knew Grey picked up on it because she laughed.

"Shit, you're so easy to read. I'm right, ain't I?"

"She just—they—" But Corey had no words.

"Uh-huh."

"Shut up." Corey tossed a dead vine at her.

"I don't know why you don't just admit it."

"Because there's nothing to admit. We're neighbors. That's all."

"I don't see you all up in arms over any of your other neighbors."

"I'm not up in arms."

"No, you just go out of your way to help that woman anytime she comes near."

"Oh, I do not."

Grey laughed again.

Corey stared her down. "Not more than I'd help anyone else."

"Uh-huh."

Corey waved her off.

"Then tell me what happened when you ushered them into the house and then drove them home."

"Nothing happened. I mean—Laken was upset and we took her inside to calm her down. End of story."

"And did it work?"

"Yes. If you must know. Actually, Whip calmed her down. He lay next to her and calmed her right down."

"And I bet Brin was especially appreciative, wasn't she?"

"As a matter of fact, she was. Laken can be a handful."

"Oh, there ain't no doubt about that, I'm sure."

"Then why the third degree?"

Grey shrugged. "Just curious is all."

"Well, stop being so damn curious."

"You kiss her yet?"

Corey stopped dead in her tracks. "I'm going to pretend you didn't even ask me that."

Grey chuckled. "You can pretend all you want. But I know you want to."

Corey bit her lip. "Where is this coming from?"

They climbed onto the Mule and headed for the stables. Ryan was outside in the corral brushing down a mare. He nodded as they approached and Corey hopped off and joined him, anxious to escape Grey.

But Grey followed her and picked up right where they left off. "Because I know you like I know the back of my hand. You like that woman."

Ryan perked up, eyed them both, but then continued his work, obviously knowing better than to interrupt. He'd learned that the hard way a time or two, and at the moment, Corey appreciated his staying out of it.

"Oh, I do not."

"Say what you want, but I can see it. And pretty soon, if you ain't careful, you'll be completely smitten."

Corey stared her down. "You're crazy."

Grey merely shook her head.

"There hasn't been anyone since Dawn, has there?" Corey asked.

"Well, no but—"

"So, I learned my lesson, did I not?"

"This woman's different."

"Yeah, she's not strung out on opioids. Thank God for that."

"No, but she's got a child. A child with special needs. Just make sure you're ready for that."

"What the hell does that mean?"

"It means you can't run if you change your mind. There's a child to consider. One who is very fond of you by the looks of things. Not to mention that they live right next door."

"What the fuck, Grey?"

"I just don't want to see you get hurt again."

"Well, maybe you should mind your own business."

Grey raised her palms. "Okay then. I've said my piece."

Corey removed her hat and ran her hand through her hair. She sighed and smacked the hat on her thigh. "Goddamn it." She walked away and headed back to the Mule. She climbed on and took off, speeding around the stables and back out through the pumpkin patch. She drove to the end of her property and found herself staring straight out at Brin's house.

She put the Mule in park and killed the engine.

"Now, why did I come here?" She leaned back and sighed. Maybe Grey was right. Maybe she was getting too involved.

But would that really be so bad?

She thought about Dawn and the hell she went through with her. All the lying and then the stealing. Dawn doing anything she could to get her fix, everyone else be damned.

It had been awful. She wouldn't wish it on her worst enemy. She knew Brin was different, very different, but trouble was trouble and Grey was right. She didn't have anywhere to run to if things got started and they didn't work out. Brin was right next door and little Laken, hell, Laken was already so taken with her. What would it do to her if she got used to having her around and then she up and disappeared from her life?

It was best to stay away. Keep things cool.

She reminded herself to thank Grey later on for the heads up. She had to be smart when it came to Brin.

Regardless of the attraction.

❖

Corey put her truck in park and adjusted her hat. Rain sprinkled down onto her windshield and the wipers stopped mid swing as she switched off the engine. She climbed from the truck and glanced up at the gray, wispy sky, allowing the cool drops to prick her skin.

It was supposed to rain the rest of the day, and she normally wouldn't mind, but she had a pumpkin patch to think of now. Too much rain could spell disaster.

"They say it's supposed to be wet the rest of the week," a meek voice said next to her.

Corey turned and saw Ivy Pettigrew standing next to her, hunched under her fancy umbrella.

"This keeps up and it's going to ruin Halloween," she continued.

Corey smiled at her and then looked back up at the clouds. "Nah, it'll be fine. Gotta have a little faith, Mrs. Pettigrew."

Ivy tsked. "I've got enough faith for the both of us, Corrina, but I'm telling you, Halloween's gonna be a wash this year."

Corey walked with her to her car. Mrs. Pettigrew was pushing ninety, but you couldn't tell by her attitude, or her spirit for that matter.

"I sure hope not," Corey said. "That would ruin the last of my pumpkin sales."

"Oh, dear," she said as they reached her car door. She looked at Corey with bright eyes. "I forgot about that."

"Hurt your peach preserve sales, too."

"I suppose it would. Things have been going well then, I take it?"

"Better than expected. Though last weekend was a little wetter than I would've liked. Your preserves are a real hit though."

"So Grey tells me."

Corey opened her car door for her and Ivy collapsed her umbrella and climbed inside.

"I'll pray for better weather," she said, offering Corey a smile.

Corey nodded. "I appreciate that."

She closed the door for her and watched as Ivy backed up and drove away.

Then Corey crossed the sidewalk to the local discount market and ducked her head to hurry inside. But just before she reached the door, she sensed someone coming out and she slammed on her brakes and looked up just in time to see Brin and Laken, shopping bags in tow.

"Hi," Brin said with a wide smile. She seemed genuinely glad to see her and Corey was equally as glad to see her, but Grey's words came to mind and she guarded her response.

"Hi. Hi, Laken."

Laken was focused on a handheld spinning fan that she controlled with a button.

"She's a bit fascinated with that thing at the moment," Brin said by way of apology.

"It does look pretty cool," Corey said.

"So how are you?" Brin asked.

"Good and you?"

"We're okay," Brin said.

They stood in silence for a moment. Then Brin spoke again. "How are the pumpkin sales going?"

"Good, real good." She sank her hands in her back pockets and tried not to stare into Brin's welcoming irises. But she was so beautiful Corey found it difficult to even breathe.

She could feel Brin's gaze searching her face, desperate for clues. When she didn't seem to find any, she continued to try at conversation.

"We just bought our costumes," she said.

Corey met her gaze, too interested not to. "Oh?"

"Uh-huh. Laken's going to be a bumble bee and I'm going to be a pirate wench."

"A pirate wench, eh?"

Brin rolled her eyes. "I wanted to be a pirate, but Laken insisted on this one." She held up the costume and Corey could only stare at it briefly because she could see right away that the dress would show ample cleavage. She felt her cheeks burning at the mere thought of Brin wearing the outfit.

She cleared her throat and prayed for calm.

It didn't come.

"Well, I'm sure you two will look great." She offered a smile. "I better be going."

She started to walk away but Brin asked another question.

"Will we be seeing you on Halloween?"

"I—sure. At some point."

"I thought we'd drop by the pumpkin patch. It's the last day it's open, isn't it?"

"Yes. Yes, it is."

"Okay then. We'll see you then." She smiled.

God, she's gorgeous.

Corey smiled but she could tell her nerves were showing. Brin seemed to pick up on it as well.

"Is everything, okay?"

"Hm? Yes. Sure. Why wouldn't it be?" She crossed her arms and then lowered them when she realized she had crossed them.

"I'm not sure. But you seem, I don't know, kind of distant."

"Distant? No, I'm just busy. Actually, came here to get my costume." She gave a nervous laugh.

"Oh? What are you going to be?"

"A—pirate." She swallowed. It was the costume she'd planned on, but now she wasn't so sure.

"You're kidding?" Brin laughed. "How funny."

"But I'm sure they're probably out by now."

"No, there are plenty." She looked down at Laken. "Hear that, Lake? Corey's gonna be a pirate!"

But Laken continued to play with her spinning fan.

Corey saw that she still had her hat on and it warmed her heart, something she noted that she could not control.

Brin looked back to Corey who stood waiting politely.

"We'll let you go then," she said. "Say bye, Laken."

"Bye," Corey said with a wave.

"See you Saturday."

Corey continued to wave.

Oh God help me.

And for the first time in days, she wished for rain.

CHAPTER TEN

Brin had mistakenly remembered Halloween to be a time of fun and carefree candy collecting. But the day had given to night, and it was quickly becoming a nightmare, and it had all started with the ever increasing rain.

Brin jerked as Laken kicked her seat again.

"Lake, please stop kicking my seat." She glanced at her in the rearview mirror. "It doesn't feel very good."

Laken whined and tugged at her costume. Her little bumble bee antennae were askew and she acted like she wanted to tear the entire thing to pieces.

"We'll change once we get home. But first we're going to Corey's."

Laken moaned and kicked some more, struggling in her booster seat.

"Here," Brin said as she dug through Laken's little jack-o'-lantern for more candy. "Have another piece of chocolate."

She kept her eyes on the road as she reached back to hand Laken the candy. Laken took it and began opening it eagerly. She stopped her fussing and ate, allowing Brin to relax some as she took the turn into Corey's.

The lot where folks parked was mostly empty and the few cars that were there were quickly being approached by people trying to escape the rainfall.

"Great, I hope we're not too late." They'd already been to town to trick-or-treat, but Brin had been anxious to get to Corey's. She wanted to say hello and let Corey check out Laken in her bumble bee costume. She looked absolutely adorable. Even if she did currently look like a bee who'd flown through a windscreen.

Brin parked and was about to kill the engine when someone pulled up next to her.

She lowered her window as she saw Corey's farmhand, Ryan, roll up in the Mule. He tipped his cowboy hat at her.

"We just closed her down, ma'am," he said.

"Oh, no. We were hoping to see Corey to wish her a happy Halloween."

"You can pull on up to the house if you like," he said. "I'm sure she'd love to see you."

"Yeah? That would be okay?"

He smiled. "I'd bet my bottom dollar." He tipped his hat again and drove away.

Brin drove slowly up to the house and killed the engine. She glanced back at Laken. "One last stop, love, and then I promise we can go home."

She unfastened her seat belt and crawled from the car. The rain was coming down good now so she got Laken out as quickly as she could and hurried her up to the front porch. Then she tried her best to straighten their costumes as they waited for the door to be answered.

"Here." She took a tissue and desperately wiped at Laken's face. The chocolate she'd eaten was somehow all over her cheeks.

"Much better."

She smiled at her and kissed her forehead. "You look absolutely adorable, you know that? Corey's gonna be so happy to see you."

The door opened and the wind kicked up, blowing rain into their backs. Brin's pirate wench skirt lifted, and she quickly tamed it down and forced a smile at a surprised-looking Corey.

"Happy Halloween!"

She tugged Laken to her and beamed proudly.

"Happy Halloween," Corey said, blinking. She removed her eyepatch as if she were embarrassed by her own costume.

"Hope we're not too late. We just wanted to come by to say hello." Brin hitched her thumb to motion behind her. "Ryan said it was okay?"

Corey stood silent for a moment and then snapped to attention. "Oh, of course. Come in, please. Get out of the rain."

They stepped into the house and Brin held Laken's wet hand. She started to fuss again at her costume as soon as Corey shut the door.

"It's really coming down," Corey said, glancing out the window. Brin noticed that Corey's pirate shirt and vest were sticking to her as if she'd been out in the rain for a while. Her feet were bare and she removed her vest and tossed it aside. It seemed they'd just come in as she was cleaning up and changing.

"I know," Brin said nervously. "We won't keep you. I'm actually a little concerned about the house." She glanced down and greeted Whip who'd just run into the room. Laken smiled as Whip licked her face.

"Oh, right. Will you be okay? They say it's only going to get worse."

Brin waved her off and Corey fingered the buttons on her white shirt. For a split second, Brin thought she might take it off. And for that split second, her heart stopped.

"Oh, we'll be fine."

Corey stared at her a moment and then hurriedly looked away. But not before Brin caught her gaze lingering over her exposed cleavage. She grinned a little, unable to help herself. It seemed the feeling was mutual. And here she thought she looked a wreck. More like a drowned sea rat than anything sexy.

Bless you, Corey Durand.

"Doesn't Laken look great?" Brin said, letting them both off the hook.

Corey smiled. "She sure does." Corey crossed over to the coffee table and retrieved a bowl of candy. She held it out to Laken. "Take your pick, kiddo. Hell, take a handful."

Laken forced her hand inside the bowl and grabbed at the candy. But instead of putting some in her jack-o'-lantern, she just kept squeezing it. Brin stepped in to help.

"Laken, put some in your pumpkin like this, remember?"

"So, she likes candy, then?" Corey asked.

"Mm-hm. But it has to be crunchy." She held up the Nestle Crunch bars. "She loves these."

"Take them all," Corey said.

"You sure?"

"If that's what she'll eat."

Brin dropped a few mini-sized bars in the jack-o'-lantern and then opened one for Laken. "Last one for tonight," she said.

"She's had a lot?"

"Oh, yeah. It's the only thing that keeps her in that costume."

"She does look cute."

"I give it another ten minutes before the bumble bee meets its maker. She is going to tear out of that thing."

Corey laughed. "What about you?"

"What about me?"

But Corey had looked away again and the blush she was sporting was more than noticeable. Even in the dim light.

"Nothing," Corey said.

A voice came from behind Corey. "I'm gonna take off."

It was Grey and she was shrugging into a long duster.

"Try to get home before it really unloads on us," Grey said.

She nodded at Brin. "Reckon you might wanna do the same. That wind's really picking up."

Brin glanced back through the window. The house shook as the wind blew more rain against the glass. The wind chimes were going nuts. "I think you're right." Suddenly, she could think of nothing but her own house. "We better go."

"You sure you'll be alright?" Corey asked.

Brin nodded, though far less sure this time.

Grey said her good-byes and walked out the door. A blast of cool, moist air infiltrated the living room.

"Do you have supplies?" Corey asked.

"Like what?"

"Flashlight, candles, radio, stuff like that."

"Somewhere." *Shit. Why do I always sound so dumb and helpless?*

"I'm still trying to unpack everything," she added, hoping it sounded reasonable.

Corey grimaced regardless. "Give me a second." She left them and Brin heard her messing around in the kitchen. She returned a few moments later with a shopping bag.

"Here. It's got most of what you need."

"Corey, I—"

"Take it. You might need it."

The lights flickered.

Brin grew uneasy. She took the bag, grateful for it.

"I'll walk you out."

Corey followed them outside and helped Laken into the car. Then she did the same for Brin.

"Please call if you need anything," she said.

Brin nodded and spoke over the wind. "I will."

Corey tapped the top of the car and backed away. Brin reversed and drove back out onto the main road. Then, as quickly and as carefully as she could, she headed for home.

❖

Brin hugged Laken tighter, pulling her closer as the wind blew and thunder growled. They'd been home for less than half an hour and the storm had only grown worse. So far, though, the house was still standing and there was only one leak in the kitchen. She could hear the drops of water falling in the designated pot as she continued to read to Laken who was somehow falling asleep through it all.

Her little eyes had drifted closed for good and Brin tucked the covers in around her and snuggled down into the bed. Laken was sleeping with her tonight. She was unwilling to risk letting her sleep on her own in the storm. She'd told herself she was doing it for Laken, but really she was doing it for herself. She didn't want to be alone and she knew she'd do nothing but worry about Laken otherwise.

She pulled the covers up around them and thought about switching off the light. As if on cue, the lights flickered and then died. The house was eerily silent save for the gusting wind. She fumbled with the grocery bag on the night table and retrieved a flashlight. She turned it on and sat very still, listening.

"Laken," she whispered.

But she was fast asleep, and Brin thanked God for small miracles. She couldn't imagine how awful things would be if Laken had been afraid of the storm. There would've been no way to help her. No way to assure her things would be okay. The wind and the thunder would've just kept coming, drowning out any security she tried to offer.

Thunder boomed and shook the house. Brin stiffened, sure Laken would wake. But she didn't.

The rain fell harder, and the wind kicked up. She sat up, knowing that something was bound to go wrong. It was just too much for the old house to handle.

She moved to the edge of the bed and slid into her slippers and housecoat, thankful they'd gone into town for those warmer pajamas. She gave Laken a concerned once-over and then headed out of the room for the kitchen. The halo of light from the flashlight led the way and she could hear the scraping of branches against the house as she slowly walked.

"Please, let everything be okay." She made it to the kitchen, what she considered to be the weakest room in the house, and looked around. The leak was worse and the drops of water had already filled the large pot she'd placed on the counter to catch them. Quickly, she dumped the water and replaced the pot. But she soon found another leak, this one closer to the window. She knelt at the kitchen cabinet to retrieve another pot and a bright flash nearly blinded her, followed by an ear-splitting boom. A loud crashing sound followed and she screamed and ducked for cover.

Cowering next to the cabinets, she scrambled for her flashlight and crawled to the adjacent wall. Wind and rain pelted her back and she turned and sat against the wall, shining the light on the ceiling of the kitchen. And there above the nook, where the bad leak had been, was a hole with a tree branch peeking through.

She scrambled to her feet as more rain fell inside and she hurried back down the hallway, worried for Laken. She slid a few times in her slippers but managed to make it back to the bedroom where Laken still lay asleep in the bed. Brin sighed with relief and hurried to her night table. Her hand shook as she fumbled once again for the contents in the grocery bag.

Quickly, she set the flashlight down upside down so its light spilled across the ceiling, allowing her a better view for lighting a candle. She got one lit and set it on the night table. Her surroundings flickered to life.

She reached for her phone and it rang in her hand, scaring her half to death. She answered it right away, just knowing it was Corey.

"Corey, oh my God, a tree branch just came through my roof!"

"A tree branch!" It wasn't Corey.

Brin looked at the caller ID. It was Miley Roberts. Her body went limp with defeat but then breathed back to life as another round of thunder sounded. At the moment, she didn't care who she was talking to. She just needed someone to hear her.

"Yes!"

"My goodness. Are you two okay?"

"Yes, we're fine. But I'm unsure what to do."

"Don't you worry your pretty little head about it. I'm calling in the calvary."

"Wait, are you sure?"

"As sure as sure can be. That's why I called you, to make sure you were okay in this storm."

She sighed. "Thank you, Miley."

"You bet. And you hang tight, sugar. We'll be right there."

They ended the call and Brin leaned back against the headboard. At least someone was coming to help.

Even if that someone was Miley Roberts.

CHAPTER ELEVEN

Miley's idea of a calvary consisted of herself and her brother, Jimmy. They arrived half an hour after Brin hung up with her, and so far, they really weren't that much help.

"There's not much we can do until daybreak," Jimmy said, shining his flashlight up at the ceiling.

"Then I feel ridiculous," Brin said. "Having you come out in the middle of the night." Thunder growled in the distance. The storm was finally moving on.

"Don't be silly," Miley said, all decked out in yellow rain gear. "We came to get you."

Brin shook her head. "What?"

"You can't stay here. It's too dangerous."

"I can't leave." She looked at the ceiling. "It's just one little area."

"Yes, but look at this mess." Miley pointed her flashlight at the strewn leaves and wet floor where the rain had blown in.

"That's easily cleaned." There was no way in hell she was leaving her house to stay with Miley Roberts. "And everywhere else is fine."

"What about little Larkin?" Miley asked.

"Laken…will be fine. She doesn't like change, so up and moving her when I absolutely don't have to would really trouble her."

Miley pressed her lips together. "I see."

"I appreciate the offer, Miley, really I do. It's just not the best idea."

"But I suppose if I was Corey Durand your answer would be different?"

"Come again?" Brin flushed with both fury and embarrassment. She prayed Miley couldn't see it.

"Never mind. Perhaps it's best if you do stay with her. She is closer after all."

"I'm not staying with anyone," Brin said.

"You're more than welcome to stay with me," Jimmy said, turning to face them. "I have plenty of room."

Brin clenched her jaw. "No. Thank you. I'm staying right here."

"He really does have a nice place," Miley said. "Perfect for children."

Brin threw up her hands. "Okay, time to get back to bed. The rain has finally stopped and I'm beat. I'll clean this up in the morning."

"I'll come by and see what all needs to be done," Jimmy said. He gave her his wide, cheesy grin. There was no doubt he was enjoying himself. He probably saw himself as her knight in shining armor.

The thought made her want to puke.

"Sure, yeah. See you tomorrow." She escorted them out.

It had been a mistake reacting the way she had with Miley on the phone. Now she was going to have to pay the price. And she was not looking forward to it.

The duo left after more reassuring on Brin's part and Brin finally closed the door and headed for the bedroom. She retrieved the burning candle and the grocery bag and set up in the kitchen, lighting two more candles to see by. Then she got busy sweeping and mopping. There was no way she could let

Laken wake up to the mess and there was no way she was going to be able to sleep. So she worked until close to dawn and then sat at the kitchen table with a nice hot cup of coffee. Thankfully, the power had come back on about an hour before.

She stared at the intruding tree branch and noted that the hole it made wasn't very large. She tried to comfort herself with that when she realized her eyes were drifting closed. When she opened them again it was after seven and she heard Laken cry out.

Quickly, she crossed to the hallway and down to the bedroom, where she saw Laken sitting up in bed. She cried out again when she saw Brin.

Brin scooped her up and carried her toward the kitchen.

"Shh, there, there. It's okay, love. You just slept in my bedroom is all." She set her down at the table and Laken rubbed her eyes. Then, when she saw the branch, she pointed.

"I know. A tree decided to pay us a visit last night. But it's okay. It's going to be fixed." Brin poured some Cheerios in Laken's little bowl. Then she got her some water, afraid the milk had probably gone bad with the lack of power.

"We'll go into town and get a few groceries later."

Laken dug into her cereal and crammed her mouth full and began to chew. She swung her feet and stared at the branch as she ate.

Brin sat across from her and sipped her reheated coffee. She reached out and touched her hand. "I'm so glad we're okay, Lake. It could've been so much worse."

Laken drank from her sippy cup and then ate some more.

Brin glanced up at the sunlight angling through the broken roof. "But it is beyond me on how I'm going to pay for all this."

The thought had come over her as she'd been cleaning. There were so many repairs that needed to be done to the house as it was, and now this. And God only knew if there was any other damage she was unaware of.

A tear slipped down her cheek as she considered it all. They just couldn't seem to catch a break.

A soft knock came from the front door. Brin looked to Laken to see if she'd heard it, but she kept eating, oblivious. It happened again and Brin sighed, not quite ready for Miley and Jimmy just yet.

She went to the door, tightening her robe just before she pulled the door open. To her surprise, she saw Corey Durand standing there, a look of genuine concern on her face.

"That tree come through your roof?" she asked.

Brin nodded, half dazed and half turned on by Corey's tight white thermal shirt and faded jeans. She was wearing a leather bomber jacket and carrying a toolbox.

Brin had to remind herself to speak. "Um, yes. It did."

Corey edged her way inside. "I thought you said you'd call me if anything happened."

Brin opened the door farther and followed her. "I didn't want to disturb you."

"You needed help," Corey said, stopping in the kitchen. "Hey, Laken."

Laken looked at her briefly and then pointed to the tree branch.

"I see that," Corey said. "Looks like you guys had a fun night."

Brin laughed. "Oh, it was barrels of fun. Dealing with Miley and Jimmy in the middle of the night is always at the top of my list of a good time."

"Miley and Jimmy?" Corey looked perplexed.

"Miley happened to call right after it happened. So she and Jimmy rushed over."

"Oh, okay."

It was obvious Corey wasn't happy, but Brin was unsure what to do about it. After all, she was the one who had to deal with them, not Corey.

"They're coming back today to help fix it."

Corey scoffed. "Jimmy Roberts?"

Brin nodded.

"Good luck with that."

"What do you mean?"

"I mean that man couldn't hang a picture, much less fix a roof."

"Oh, no." Brin sank into a kitchen chair. "Then why did he say he would help?"

"Do I really have to explain that to you?" Corey asked. She came closer and looked straight up into the hole.

"No, I suppose not."

"Uh-huh. My guess is he's got only one thing on his mind and it ain't this roof."

"You don't have to be so crass," Brin said, cringing.

"It's true, isn't it? I've known that man a long time and know his game well. He'll say and do whatever he has to to get close to a woman. But it's usually not long before they figure out he's full of nothing but hot air."

"I know that, Corey. Trust me, I know. But honestly, I need all the help I can get. I don't even know how I'm going to pay for all this."

Corey watched her closely and her face softened. "I didn't mean to upset you."

"You guys all come rushing in here to help and I don't even know if I can afford the help."

Corey sank down into the chair next to her. "Hey, it's okay. It's really not that bad."

"Corey, I have a hole in my roof!"

"It can be fixed."

"And God knows what else."

"I'll go up and take a look, okay?"

Another knock came from the front door and Brin slumped, knowing who it was. She crossed to the door and answered it. Miley was all smiles, dressed in denim overalls and a ball cap. Her lipstick was brighter than the morning sun.

"Good morning, sunshine," she said, opening the screen door. She edged her way inside and Jimmy followed close behind, also dressed in head to toe denim, though he had on a denim shirt and jeans. Even so, he still looked far from a handyman with his slicked back hair and freshly shaved jaw. His flashy gold watch didn't help matters any.

Brin followed them into the kitchen where they both stared at Corey, who had stood to gather her toolbox.

"Why, Corey Durand. What a surprise to see you here so bright and early," Miley said.

"Not really, Miley. I am her neighbor you know."

"Yes, but I was under the assumption that she wasn't going to call you."

"She didn't. I was driving by and saw the damage myself."

"So, you thought you'd what? Help?" She eyed the toolbox.

Corey grinned and Brin could tell that it was forced. "That was the idea."

"Well, we've got it under control," Jimmy said.

"Do you now?"

Corey stared him down.

"Corey offered to take a look," Brin said, feeling the growing tension.

"No need," Jimmy said. "I got it."

"Jimmy's got it," Miley said.

"Since when?" Corey asked. "Last I heard Jimmy couldn't tell a hammer from a nail."

Jimmy returned the forced grin. "Well, you heard wrong."

Corey grabbed her toolbox. "Brin, what do you want?"

Brin blinked rapidly, more confused than ever.

"We've already got the lumber and everything needed to fix you right up," Miley said.

"Miley, guys, everyone just wait. I need to sit down and think. I don't know how I'm going to pay for all this."

"Oh, don't worry about that, Brin," Miley said. "Jimmy and I got you covered."

Brin didn't like the sound of that. It made her feel like there were definitely going to be strings attached and it made her stomach churn with nerves.

Why did this have to happen now of all times?

Laken shoved her bowl onto the floor and Miley jerked from the noise.

"Oh, my God, that scared me!" She clutched her chest. "No, no Larkin. Don't do that."

Brin picked up the bowl and took it to the sink. Then she scooped Laken up into her arms.

"Her name is LAKEN. Not Larkin. And please do not discipline her. I will take care of that."

Miley rubbed her throat. "Well."

"And as for this roof thing, I need time to think. So, if you could all just go for now I'd really appreciate it."

"But—" Jimmy started.

"Please," Brin said, walking them all toward the door.

"I'll call you all later."

Corey clenched her jaw but didn't say a word. Brin was grateful. She didn't have the strength to argue with her and she knew what she was going to say.

Miley and Jimmy weren't to be trusted.

Brin knew it and she could feel it.

But she also had feelings to contend with over Corey. And those, at the moment, felt riskier than anything Miley and Jimmy could throw at her.

CHAPTER TWELVE

"Tara, hi. It's Corey Durand." Corey pulled into a parking space in front of Flick's Hardware and put the truck in park. She'd just dropped off Ryan at the drugstore and she'd purposely waited to make this phone call in private.

"Corey Durand? Well, to what do I owe the pleasure?"

Corey chuckled softly at her seductive sounding voice.

"I was actually calling in a favor."

"For you? Anything."

"No, seriously."

"I am being serious. Serious as a heart attack."

Corey chose to ignore her and move right on to the topic at hand. "I hope you don't mind, but I gave your number to a new friend of mine. She has a four-year-old niece who may benefit from your expertise."

"Oh?"

"Yes. So, I just wanted to give you a heads up in case she calls. So far she's been a bit hesitant."

"What's her name?"

"Brin. And her niece is Laken."

"Oh, I actually just spoke to her this morning. Real intense, kind of hyper?"

"Brin? Yes."

Tara laughed. "She sounded pretty worried. Asked me all kinds of questions. It took me a while before I could convince her to bring Laken in for an evaluation."

"But she is coming, right?"

"She has an appointment."

"Great. Thank you. Thanks so much."

"What's the deal with her? I mean, why the heavy interest on your part?"

Corey paused and looked at herself in the rearview mirror. "Let's just say I really think you can help them."

"Okay, well, you got it. Of course you know once they come in I won't be able to discuss the treatment or anything with you."

"I'm aware. I'm just glad they're coming in."

"So, what about you, Corey? You seeing anyone?"

Corey grinned, embarrassed. She stared down at her jeans and picked at a loose thread. "No."

"I didn't think so. I think I'd hear about something like that."

"With Miley Roberts around, I'm sure you would have."

"How is little miss perfect anyway?"

"Same."

"Ugh. Say no more. But if you ever change your mind and want to go out, you better call me."

Corey laughed. "I'll talk to you later, Tara."

"Alright. And hey, thanks for the rec."

"You bet. Bye."

They ended the call and Corey climbed from the truck and headed into Flick's Hardware.

Flick was behind the counter talking to a customer Corey didn't recognize. So she made her way down the appropriate aisle for roofing nails and shingles. Though she hadn't spoken to Brin since the day before about her roof, she wanted to be prepared to help her should she need her. And since it appeared that Jimmy Roberts was going to be on the job, or at least lingering, that help would be needed sooner rather than later.

She still hadn't gotten over seeing his fancy truck pulled beside Brin's house earlier that morning when she and Ryan had driven by. She'd thought Brin was going to call before she accepted any help from anyone. It seemed that was no longer the case. She just hoped Brin knew what the hell she was doing in allowing Jimmy to fix her roof.

Corey stopped in front of the area where Flick kept his shingles and nails and roofing tar. Almost all of it was gone.

"Help you, Corey?" Flick said as he ambled down the aisle.

She pointed. "Where's all your roofing supplies?"

He sank a hand in his vest pocket. "Jimmy Roberts come in here recently and damn near bought the place out."

"All of it?"

"This is all I've got left."

Corey knelt, examined what little was there and stood, shaking her head.

"Damn it. He has no idea what he's doing."

"I heard he was fixing that new gal's roof. Your new neighbor."

"He sure thinks he is."

Flick rubbed his stubbled jaw. "Yeah, I've never known that boy to fix much of anything."

"Me neither."

"Hope he knows what he's doing."

"He doesn't."

Corey tugged on the bill of her ball cap and sighed. "I'll take what you got left here. And some lumber in the back."

"Just got in a new shipment."

"Thank God for that."

"What's going on?" Ryan asked as he came up behind Flick.

Flick turned and placed a hand on his shoulder in a welcoming gesture. Ryan greeted him with a smile and opened his bottle of Mountain Dew for a hearty swig.

"Jimmy Roberts is what's up," Corey said.

"What now?" Ryan asked.

"Well, look." She pointed at the remaining supplies.

Ryan's eyebrows shot up.

"Damn," he said. "He bought all that for that one hole?"

"Guess so."

"Oh, and not just that. He bought lots of lumber and a ladder too. If I didn't dislike the son of a bitch so much, I'd been singing his praises. But as it was, I just thought he'd lost his mind in buying so much. Course it helped my pocketbook too."

"No one's faulting you, Flick. You're just doing your job."

"Well, I feel might bad about it, Corey. You being stuck with what little is left. I've got an order put in. Course I got two other people waiting on it too. Jimmy beat everyone in here the morning after the storm."

"That's okay, Flick. I'll make do."

"Those other folks will probably go down to the huge orange o'porium. Can't says I blame 'em. Damn Jimmy Roberts. If he cost me customers—"

Corey patted his shoulder. "I'm sure he didn't, Flick. Don't worry about that. Just get your shelves restocked. That's all you can do."

Flick continued to bad-mouth Jimmy as Corey and Ryan carried the goods up to the counter. Then Ryan drove the truck around back to load up the lumber. Corey climbed in and secured her seat belt, content with letting Ryan drive.

"Why did you buy all that?" he asked. "Didn't Grey tell you to let it go?"

He was referring to the conversation she'd had with Grey that morning. One in which Grey made it clear that she should stay away and let Jimmy fix that roof if that's what Brin wanted.

Corey had argued that she really didn't believe that that was what Brin wanted, but Grey countered with a good point. Brin had never called her back to tell her what she wanted. And Jimmy's truck in her drive suggested she'd made up her mind.

But Corey still didn't feel right about it. So she couldn't let it go.

"Grey doesn't always know what's best for folks," Corey said.

Ryan chewed his lower lip, obviously choosing not to argue though he probably could have.

Corey narrowed her eyes at him after examining his bag from the drugstore. Save for some gum and the Mountain Dew he was drinking, it looked empty.

"Did you get 'em?" she asked.

Ryan glanced at her and then back to the road. "Uh, no."

"Why not?"

He squeezed the steering wheel as if he were nervous. "I'm not sure what to get."

"What do you mean?"

"I don't know." He shrugged. "There are so many to choose from. How do I know what to get?"

Corey closed her eyes. "Go back to the drugstore."

"What?"

"Go back."

"But, Corey—"

"Just do it."

Ryan slowed the truck and did a U-turn. Then he pulled into the drugstore parking lot. They sat in the truck for a moment with the engine idling.

Corey spoke. "I'm going to go in there and—"

"Thank you, Corey, thank you!" He clasped his hands together and gave her a pleading look.

She stopped him. "I'm not getting them *for* you. I'm just going to go in there to look and tell you what to go get."

Ryan lowered his hands. Corey crawled from the truck and headed inside. She made her way down the aisle and stopped in front of the condoms. Ryan had been right. There were a lot to choose from. But hell if she knew. She examined a few boxes and nodded hello at a few passersby. They looked surprised to see her looking at the prophylactics, but she didn't care. She had to do this for the kid.

Ryan was like a son to her and she wasn't about to let him down.

She made her way back outside and climbed in the truck.

"Second row down, the green box on the far right."

Ryan stared at her.

"What?" she asked.

"What about the cashier? Is it…you know…a woman?"

Corey took her hat off and scratched her head. "Ryan, listen. If you're not mature enough to buy the damn things, then you're not mature enough to have sex."

He lowered his head. "Yeah. I reckon you're right."

"Do you like this girl?"

"I—" He looked up at her. "I love her, Corey."

"Then get your ass in there and buy those condoms."

She tugged on his cowboy hat playfully and slugged his arm. He exited the truck without another word and walked solemnly up to the drugstore. When he emerged again, his face was bright red, but he had a big grin on his face.

Corey gave his arm a squeeze and let him have his pride as they drove the rest of the way home in silence. They didn't speak a word until they came upon Brin's house around the turn where Jimmy's truck was pulling out.

He about ran them off the road he was driving so fast.

"Whoa, there, mister," Ryan said, swerving a little. "What's his hurry?"

"That's just Jimmy. Thinks he owns the road."

Corey eyed Brin's house as they approached. "Slow down a little."

She scanned the roof and saw where Jimmy had removed the tree limb and patched up the roof with lumber. It looked as though he'd yet to finish the job though.

"Pull up to the side of the house."

"What for?"

"So I can get a look at the tree."

Ryan eased onto the gravel drive and put the truck in park. Corey exited the truck with Ryan close behind.

"Aren't we going to get in trouble?"

Corey walked right up to the tree. "Nah, doesn't look like she's home."

Ryan still looked around as if he were uneasy.

"Relax, kid, we're looking at a tree, not breaking in the house."

Corey examined the old oak and saw where the lightning had hit it. Then she noted how close what remained was to the house. It looked as though Jimmy had cut away the offending branch, but he'd done nothing else to prune the tree back and the lightning had nearly split the damn thing in two.

"This tree needs to come down," Corey said. "The sooner the better."

"You gonna tell her that?"

"Someone needs to. Might as well be me. If not, the next storm that comes through is gonna cause a whole lot more trouble."

"You gonna offer to cut it down for her?"

Corey shoved on the trunk, getting a feel for its sturdiness. "I might do. Why? You wanna help?"

"Sure, why not? She seems nice enough."

"She can be."

"Then why doesn't Grey like her?"

Corey gave the tree one last glance and then headed for the truck. Ryan was right on her heels.

"Because it's like I said, kid. Grey doesn't always know what's best for folks."

CHAPTER THIRTEEN

The drive to Flagstaff took about forty minutes, and thankfully, Laken was calm and content to stare out the window. Brin, on the other hand, was a nervous wreck.

"We're here," she said as she slowed and pulled into a strip mall. She found the Sensory Path sign and parked nearby. Her heart rate had doubled and she had to wipe the sweat from her hands on her jeans. She said a silent prayer before she climbed from the car and got Laken.

She really needed for everything to go right and for Laken to somehow be okay, whatever that was. What she needed was a miracle.

Laken climbed from the car without a fight and walked with her up to the doors. Brin could already see and hear children laughing and playing inside. She supposed that was a good sign.

"Okay, love," Brin said, kneeling in front of Laken. "We're gonna go in here and check this place out, okay? How does that sound?"

Laken didn't respond and she didn't give her any eye contact. Brin took a deep breath and opened the door and stepped inside, Laken's hand in hers.

They walked up to a large counter and Brin spoke to the young woman behind the desk.

"Hi, I'm Brin and this is my niece, Laken. We have a three o'clock appointment with Tara."

"Brin?"

Brin turned and saw a woman with short auburn hair walking toward her with a smile. She extended her hand.

"Tara," she said.

"Hi," Brin said. "And this is Laken."

Tara smiled down at Laken and knelt before her. "Hiya, Laken. I'm Tara." She held out her hand but got no response. "I like your hat," she said.

She straightened and spoke to Brin. "That's one of Corey's hats, isn't it?"

"It is," Brin said. "Laken wears it everywhere. She really likes Corey."

Tara smiled. "What's not to like? Corey is pretty special."

Brin burned at the comment as jealousy rushed through her. She had no idea where it came from and she fought against it, hoping Tara didn't notice.

What is my problem?

"You know Corey well, then?" Brin couldn't help but ask.

"Oh, Corey and I go way back." She winked at her and Brin boiled.

"Oh."

Tara didn't seem to notice. Instead she focused on Laken. "You okay with leaving her with me for about an hour?"

No. No, I'm not okay with that. Right now I want to slap that sexy little grin off your face. But you're the only one I know of who can help me with Laken. So...

"Yes. That will be fine."

"Great. There's a Bun Huggers next door if you're up for a burger or just working on your laptop. Most of our parents hang out there until the session is finished."

"Okay." Brin felt more at ease knowing she would be right next door. She kissed Laken on the cheek. "Be good. I'll just be right next door."

She straightened, forced a smile at Tara, who was already holding Laken's hand, and walked out of the building. The cold wind bit at her flesh as she headed for the burger joint. She could smell the burgers cooking before she even pulled open the door. As delicious as they smelled, however, she was too nervous to eat, so she bought a soda and sat at one of the empty booths. She eyed her phone as it alerted her to a text message.

To her surprise, she saw it was from Corey.

Corey: *Is Jimmy planning on doing anything about that oak tree that was hit next to your house?*

Brin grimaced. What? No hello or how are you? Just Jimmy and the tree?

Brin: *IDK*

Corey: *Well, has he mentioned it?*

Brin: *No. Why?*

Corey: *It needs to come down. The wind alone could knock it down at this point.*

What?

Brin wanted to roll her eyes. Jimmy had said he had cut the tree back and that everything was fine. Besides, what did Corey care? And more importantly, how did she know about the current status of the tree?

Brin: *Were you at my house?*

Corey: *Checking out the tree.*

Brin: *Why?*

Corey: *Because it's dangerous and I was worried Jimmy wouldn't take care of it. Seems I was right.*

Brin: *He said he cut it back and it's fine.*

Corey: *Not good enough. Better I do it. He doesn't know what he's doing.*

Brin pushed out a breath. Funnily enough, Jimmy had been saying similar things about Corey. What was the deal with the two of them? And how did she end up in the middle?

Corey: *Thanks for the phone call, BTW. You could've told me you'd decided on Jimmy.*

Brin felt her eyes widen. She texted back so hard her thumbs hurt.

Brin: *I didn't get a chance! I showed up from a trip into town to find him working on my roof and Miley waiting on the porch with a casserole. They just insisted.*

Corey: *You still could've said no.*

Brin: *I don't have to answer to you or anyone.*

Corey: *Ok. But know it's not a good idea.*

Brin: *Well, right now they're the only ones being even remotely polite to me. So I guess I'll stick with them.*

Brin waited for a response. She didn't get one and she fumed so hard she could almost feel the steam coming from her ears.

She sat and stared at her phone for the next half hour, coming up with all sorts of things to say but not having the nerve to say any of them. What gave Corey the right? What gave Jimmy the right? What was it about her that these two were competing to fix her house and not give one damn about how she felt about it?

She scrolled down her list of contacts and saw Miley's name. She so badly wanted to text her to say the whole thing was off. But she thought of all the work Jimmy had already done and about that casserole still sitting in her fridge. It was a nice gesture and suddenly she was so tired she couldn't even imagine fixing dinner. It would be nice just to heat up that casserole. How did Miley always know exactly what to do to get her way?

She eyed the time and made her way back to the Sensory Path.

Tara was waiting for her next to the ball pit. She pointed and Brin caught sight of Laken walking on what looked like waterbed mattresses on the floor. She was barefoot and walking very carefully, heels down. When she reached the ball pit, she jumped inside and played. Then she emerged with two balls, one in each hand.

She followed Tara and then ran up to Brin and held up the balls.

"Great job," Brin said, loving how happy Laken seemed.

Tara placed her hand on Laken's shoulder. "Laken, go ahead and go play. I'm going to talk to your aunt for a little while." Then she motioned for another woman to come lead Laken back into the makeshift play area.

"Would you care to sit in my office?"

"Sure."

Tara led the way and Brin sat across from her desk. Tara settled in and tucked short strands of hair behind her triple pierced ears. It seemed to be a well-practiced gesture, as if maybe her hair had been longer at one point. The thought did little to comfort Brin. Tara was an attractive woman, and would be with long or short hair, and she wondered if Corey thought the same.

"So? What's the verdict?" Brin felt her stomach flip as she waited.

Tara steepled her fingers and smiled. It looked genuine.

"I don't think she's autistic."

A huge breath escaped Brin and she almost cried with relief. "Oh, thank God." She wiped a stray tear and gathered herself as Tara continued.

"I think her issues are sensory."

"Are you sure? I mean, that she's not autistic? I've only ever been told to label her and drug her up."

Tara held up her hands. "I've seen a lot of kids, Brin. And I really don't think she is."

This time Brin did cry. Tara passed her a tissue.

"I think it's all sensory."

"And you're a what? An occupational therapist? She's seen two of you before at the behest of a neurologist and they didn't come to the same conclusion."

"They probably didn't spend enough time one-on-one with her. I spent close to two hours with her and she did things my autistic kids can't do. But…" She held up her hands. "Only time will tell what her progress will be."

Brin deflated. "What does that mean?"

"It means that she needs therapy. Here at my facility, three days a week, for at least a few hours at a time."

"Oh, God. Okay." She shifted. "Do you take insurance?"

"Yes. We also have payment plans."

"Okay."

"But she needs to start right away. The sooner the better. We need to get her talking and engaging."

"And eating normally."

Tara laughed. "Yes, that too."

"What kind of things will you be doing with her?"

"Well, what you saw earlier was what we use to correct the toe-walking. The kids walk on the waterbeds, which they're unable to toe-walk on, and their reward is the ball pit."

"She seemed to like that."

"She liked everything we did today." She stood and opened a cabinet behind her desk. She pulled out a set of large earphones. "She'll have homework too."

"Okay."

Tara handed them over. "These are for her music therapy. You'll put these on her and play a classical song on low volume while she's doing things around the house. I want you to speak to her while she's wearing them and engage with her every so often. This will encourage her to either focus on the music or focus on you."

"I see."

"Her time with me will be spent focusing on her sensory needs. I need to discover just where her issues stem from and work from there. So far, I've figured out that she doesn't like mushy or soft food. So it's an issue with her mouth. But I need to further investigate whether or not it's the roof of her mouth, her lips, the inside of her cheeks, or maybe all of the above."

"And how can you help her with that?"

Tara opened a drawer and pulled out a rubbery thimble with pointed edges. "I desensitize her with this soft thimble by massaging the inside of her mouth and lips and then reward her with something she likes."

"Wow."

"Seems so simple, right?"

"Actually, it does. And this is going to be the cure to bringing her out of her shell?"

"You're going to be shocked at how well she does."

"I'm already shocked. I can't believe how well she's interacted here today already."

"We're looking for a pathway into Laken's mind. And once we find it, she's going to come to life and thrive."

Brin teared up again.

"In the meantime," Tara said, "I also think it's a good idea for you to enroll her in the local preschool. We need to get her talking and engaging with other children her own age. So on the days she isn't here, she should be in school."

"Okay. I can do that." Brin blotted her cheek with a tissue. "Will she…you know, be able to start school on time? You know, kindergarten?"

"I don't see why not. Of course it will depend on her progress, but I don't see anything getting in her way."

"And you really think she's okay?"

Tara laughed softly. "I think she's going to be fine."

She seemed to wait for Brin to settle down some before she spoke again. "I know some of your story from our phone conversation and from your paperwork, but would you mind telling me a little more?"

"Ask away," Brin said, balling up the tissue.

"How has Laken reacted to her mother's death? Have you noticed behavior changes or her grieving?"

Brin thought for a moment. "Laken was pretty much like this when Breana was alive. So when Breana got sick, Laken just kind of adapted. She would sit at Breana's bedside and color in her book or watch television. We would explain to her that Mommy was sick and that Mommy didn't feel good, but Laken didn't show any reaction."

"What about when Breana passed?"

"Same. Laken was in her own little world. I would try things, like sitting with her with Breana's picture and explain to her that Mommy had died and that she wasn't coming home, but that it was going to be okay because I was there with her."

"How often did you do that?"

"Every day for the first month."

"Good, that's good."

"But Laken rarely engaged. And when she did it was so quick I almost thought I imagined it."

"What did she do?"

"She would, and still does, bring the photo to me and sit with me. And that's when she does it. She points. She points at

Breana and then looks up at me, as if asking me to tell her about her. But then just as quickly, she's back in her little shell."

"Mm. Okay. How often does she bring you the photo now?"

"Once a week, maybe."

"Okay. Keep doing what you're doing. But also talk about Breana even when you aren't looking at the photo. As Laken begins to communicate more, you want to let her know that talking about her mother is okay."

Brin nodded.

"What about her father? Is he in the picture?"

"No. He's never had any interest in her. Left my sister as soon as he found out she was pregnant."

"I see. Well, is there anyone else in her life that she engages with on a regular basis?"

Brin shifted in her seat. "Uh, yes. She seems to like Corey Durand a whole lot."

Tara blinked as if surprised. "Oh, okay."

"You seem surprised."

"I just—Corey's pretty great. I can see why Laken would take to her."

"Yes, well…not sure how much of her we'll be seeing here in the near future. I think she's upset with me."

"Corey? Now that does surprise me." She winked. "Corey's got a huge heart. Given enough time, you'll see that, if you haven't already."

"You're really fond of her, aren't you?" Brin couldn't help herself, she could see it all over her face.

"I am."

Brin cleared her throat and after a moment, Tara stood and rounded the desk. Brin exited the office before her. "It was very nice meeting you and I look forward to working with you and Laken both." She shook Brin's hand and motioned for the woman to bring Laken to the door. She already had her shoes on, and once again Brin was amazed. Laken was allowing people to do things she'd only ever let Brin or Breana do.

"Me too," Brin said. "And thank you again."

Tara waved and walked away, leaving Brin alone and fuming with jealousy once again, despite her growing fondness for her.

CHAPTER FOURTEEN

You ain't said much these days," Grey said as she and Corey tossed straw up onto one of the two platforms in the barn.

"Maybe I ain't got much to say," Corey said as she forked more straw. They were preparing the goats for a cold winter and Corey was keeping quiet, not really having anything to say that Grey would want to hear.

"That's a little unusual," Grey said.

Wiley, one of the goats, jumped up onto the platform and made himself at home on the fresh straw, while the rest were content feeding on the silage she and Grey had just provided.

Grey chuckled as Corey forked more straw and tossed it right on top of him. Wiley didn't seem to mind and Corey didn't feel like wrestling him off the platform. He did get his name honestly after all.

"As I was saying. It's a little unusual you being so quiet and all," Grey continued.

Corey kept working, starting in on the other platform. The goats kept warm by sleeping off the ground and the straw added extra insulation to the already well-insulated barn. She cared a lot about her animals so she always went the extra mile to make sure they were cared for. And that meant insulating the barn and providing plenty of straw for added warmth.

"How's that little girl doing?" Grey finally asked as she finished with Wiley's platform and joined in to help Corey with the other.

"Who?"

"You know who. Don't play dumb. It doesn't become you."

"If you mean Laken, I have no idea. I assume she's doing fine."

"You haven't spoken to Brin?" Grey asked, stopping her movement.

Corey frowned. "Not a word."

"Well, why not?"

This time Corey stopped moving. "What's it to you? You're the one who didn't want me talking to her in the first place."

Grey stabbed her pitchfork into the ground and leaned on it. "Now hold on a second. I didn't say anything of the sort. I just told you to be careful and to not fret over fixing that roof of hers if she was happy having Jimmy fix it."

"Yeah, okay. Admit it. You were more than glad when she chose Jimmy."

"Is that what's eating you? That she chose Jimmy over you?"

Corey tossed her pitchfork and sank down on the platform. She yanked off her hat and scratched her head. "Well, yeah, as a matter of fact, it upsets me. I mean, why him?"

"You mean why not you?"

"Yes! I've done nothing but help her and that's how she acts?"

"Maybe it's because you have helped her so much. Maybe she feels bad about it. Didn't want to put you out again."

"But Jimmy Roberts? Come on, Grey. The guy's a tool."

Grey laughed. "I'm not sure what that means but it seems fitting."

"I'm serious."

"You're really hurt over this, ain't ya?"

Corey sighed. "I just don't understand."

"Well, maybe it's for the best, if you're feeling this strongly about it."

"What does that mean?"

"Means maybe you feel more for her than you've admitted to yourself. In which case, I'm damn glad you're staying away."

"She's not Dawn, Grey. Not every woman is Dawn."

Grey sat down next to her. "Do you realize that up until two months ago those words would've never come out of your mouth?"

Corey cocked her head.

"Your tune didn't change until that cute little blonde moved in with her niece."

"Come on, Grey, I'm not in love with her or anything."

"Maybe not. But you are having feelings."

Corey threw up her hands. "So what's wrong with feelings? If that was what I was having, that is."

"Nothing. Especially if they are for an appropriate person."

"Appropriate?"

"One who doesn't have her plate full with a new child and a house that's falling down around her. And let's not forget that you know very little about her. Do you even know what she does for a living?"

Corey opened her mouth to speak but couldn't.

"And there's also the fact that she's letting a man like Jimmy Roberts come around. So maybe she ain't as gay as we thought."

"No, she's gay. She told me flat out. And she's not into Jimmy at all."

"Then what gives?"

Corey shrugged. "She said he and Miley just kept showing up uninvited so she caved."

Grey reached in her back pocket and pulled out a folded bag of sunflower seeds. She shoved some in her mouth and worked them a bit before she continued.

"That does sound like Jimmy and Miley. But even so, it sounds fishy. Letting those two around for company can't be a good thing."

"They're just full of themselves," Corey said. "They aren't criminals or anything. And Brin's new here. And alone. She probably just appreciates the help."

"You still standing up for her, ain't ya?"

"I'm a little confused as to why you're not. You're acting like Brin is a criminal."

Grey spit out some shells. "You got hurt real bad, Corey. And that hurt went on for years. I saw you suffer through it. So, I'm a little protective now."

"Brin's not like that."

"You don't know what she's like."

"Not totally. But I know she's not like Dawn."

"I hope another woman like that never comes near you."

Corey placed her hat back on her head. "I do too, Grey. But we can't go around assuming every woman I come into contact with is just like her. That's no way to live."

Grey wrapped an arm around her. "Boy, how you've changed. Guess I better catch up to you, huh?"

"Please."

"Alright. But only on one condition."

"What's that?"

"You be careful with this Brin."

"Grey, come on!"

"I mean it. Just use caution."

"Fine."

Grey smiled and Corey knocked off her cowboy hat with a hearty laugh.

Grey chased it down before a goat got to it and they finished with the straw and the feed. They rode back through the ranch together in the Mule with the wind nipping at their skin, trying to get through their clothes.

"Storm's a brewing," Grey said, pointing at the sky. "Anything else need to get done before it hits?"

Corey eyed the darkening clouds. "We need to check on the horses again. The thunder really traumatized Lily last time."

They rode over to the stable and climbed off the Mule. Ryan was already inside, working with Lily. Several horses nodded and neighed, already feeling the storm moving in.

"How's she doing?" Corey asked, leaning on the stall door.

Ryan tightened Lily's thunder jacket and rubbed her down. "She won't eat. She knows it's coming."

"They all do."

"Speaking of that, anyone seen Whip?" Corey asked.

Ryan spoke. "He's already in the house, pacing and whining. Saw him on my way out here."

Corey rubbed her temple. "That poor dog hates storms worse than Lily. I better get his thunder jacket on him, too." Whip had been afraid of storms since he was a pup. Corey had no rhyme or reason for it.

"Hopefully, it won't thunder much," Grey said. "Just calling for a lot of sleet."

"I sure hope it's not a bad one," Corey said.

Ryan glanced over at her. "We never did cut that tree down over at Brin's."

"No, we didn't."

"Should we go try and do it real quick?"

Corey felt Grey's eyes on her. "I'll let Jimmy handle it."

"But you said—"

"I know what I said, kid. But I can't help her if she doesn't want it."

Ryan continued to rub down Lily and Corey tried to give her a carrot. She refused it.

"She's too nervous," Ryan said.

I am too. I'm worried about that damn tree. I sure hope the storm doesn't bring much wind.

"Well, I'm gonna take off," Grey said as she walked down the line of stalls, checking on each horse. "Everything looks good here."

Corey gave her a wave. "See ya."

"See ya," Grey said as she left them behind.

Ryan spoke softly to Lily as he continued to try to relax her.

"You sure about that tree?" he asked softly. "Grey's gone. We can go cut it down real quick."

Corey sighed. "It's a good idea, kid, it is. But truth be told, I don't think Brin wants us there."

He blinked at her. "Why not?"

Corey shrugged. "I guess because she's having Jimmy take care of it all."

"That's crazy," he said. "That guy…" He shook his head.

"You ain't got to tell me twice."

He laughed. "You sound like Grey."

"I do, don't I?"

"Where is she from anyhow?"

"Grey? North Carolina."

He nodded. "I figured it was somewhere in the South."

"She makes a mean pecan pie."

"That she does," he said. "And she sure is protective of you."

He grabbed a brush and began brushing Lily down, all the while whispering softly to her. Ryan was so good with horses that folks around town called him the horse whisperer. It was truly a gift and one he'd had since he was a young boy.

"Can I ask you something, Corey?"

Corey straightened. "Depends."

"Why doesn't she want you around Brin?"

Corey chewed on her lower lip.

"Is it because of your ex-girlfriend?"

"What do you know about my ex-girlfriend?"

He shrugged. "I can remember her and all, but I just remember her disappearing a lot and causing trouble. But people have said things. You know, around town."

"Ah, hell, really?"

"It is a small town, Corey."

"I realize that, but I hate gossip. It does nothing but cause trouble."

He shrugged again. "So you gonna tell me?"

"Grey doesn't want me to get hurt again."

"So the rumors are true, then? Your ex was…bad?"

"She got mixed up with drugs."

"Oh. Like my uncle Trent?"

Corey nodded.

"But Brin's not into drugs, is she?"

"No."

"Then what's the big deal? I mean, she seems nice. And she's pretty and you obviously like her."

"Now, how do you know that?"

He grinned sheepishly. "Because you're always trying to help her and stuff. You've, you know, kind of come out of your shell around her."

"Oh, really?"

"Yeah, and I'm not the only one who thinks so either. Everyone around town…" He blushed as if he'd said too much.

"Rumors? About Brin and me?"

He nodded.

Corey pushed away from the stall. "Nothing has even happened!"

Lily neighed and Ryan soothed her.

"I'm sorry, Corey, but it's what people are saying."

"What are they saying exactly?"

"That you've got it bad for the new woman in town."

Corey closed her eyes.

Could this be why Jimmy and Miley are putting on the full-court press? Could it be why Brin is letting them?

Corey pushed away from the stall again. "You finish up and go on home, ya hear? I don't want you caught up in this storm."

"Sure thing, boss. And hey, I'm sorry if I said anything that upset you," he called out to her.

She raised her hand as she walked away. "It's not you I'm mad at, kid. It's this damn town."

CHAPTER FIFTEEN

Brin hugged herself as she walked down the hallway to check on Laken. Outside, the storm was kicking up and the temperature had dropped several degrees, leaving a noticeable chill in the house. She stopped at the thermostat and adjusted the heat, hoping it would help sooner rather than later.

She continued on into Laken's room and found her asleep in her bed with her large headphones on. She'd really taken to the music therapy, and she liked to wear the headphones on her own time, loving the classical music. She especially loved falling asleep with the music on at night. Brin approached her quietly and removed the headphones, careful not to wake her. She switched off the low-playing music and tucked Laken's covers up around her. Then she sat on the edge of the bed and stroked her hair. She could still smell the baby shampoo she'd used to bathe her with, and her little cheek felt warm against the back of her fingers. A tear slipped down her face as she sat and stared at her. Boy, how things had changed within the span of a year.

She never could've imagined losing her sister. Never could've imagined raising Laken on her own. But here she was, her reality a strong slap to the face. Was she doing a good enough job? Would Breana be proud? Was Laken happy?

She wiped away another tear and kissed Laken on the forehead.

"I love you," she whispered. "More than you'll ever know."

She extinguished the bedside light and made sure her night light was on. Then she rose and pulled the door slightly closed before heading back down the hallway. Beyond the walls, the wind roared, and she could hear the smattering of rain as it began to beat against the house. She crossed to the kitchen and made herself some cinnamon tea before settling in in the living room with her laptop. She had a ton of work to catch up on and there was no time like the present.

She pulled a throw over her legs and switched on her computer. As the rain and wind assaulted the house, she hoped with everything she had that the house would hold up. But as she set in to work, Corey's words about Jimmy Roberts kept replaying in her mind.

❖

Brin awoke to a loud crash. She tossed her laptop aside on the couch and ripped away the throw covering her legs. Panicked, she darted into the kitchen, unsure where the noise came from. She slid to a stop as her stocking-covered feet hit icy cold water. She yelped and switched on the light. A layer of water covered the kitchen floor and her gaze moved upward, searching for the source of the leak. There, on the ceiling, it was. Water came in in large droplets, falling to the floor, the ceiling already stained and bulging from the buildup.

"Goddammit!" But her mind went back to the crash she'd heard. She ran down the hallway and checked on Laken. She found her fast asleep, so she hurried back to the living room and unlocked the front door. She grabbed the nearby flashlight, one of the ones Corey had given her, and stepped outside onto the lit porch. Icy wind and rain attacked her, and she winced from the shock of the chill. Covering her face as best she could, she walked to the edge of the porch and scanned her driveway for the tree. But it was nowhere to be found.

Confused, she hurried down the porch steps and walked across the gravel to the car. There, just on the other side, was the tree. It had cracked and fallen and just missed her vehicle by inches.

She stood and stared, studying how lucky she'd been the wind hadn't been blowing the other direction. If it had, the tree would've come down on the house, just like Corey had said. As it was, it was bad enough and she knew she'd hear from Corey about it.

Damn Jimmy. He'd told her it would be fine. That he took care of it.

He also said that about the roof.

Fuck.

Now what?

She hugged herself as the cold penetrated again and she rushed back inside. She bolted the door behind her and crossed to her bedroom to change clothes. Then, wearing her sneakers, she went back into the kitchen and retrieved the large pots and buckets once again. She sighed as she placed them underneath the leaks and then got out the mop.

It was going to be a very long night.

❖

Brin awoke to the noise of a scooting chair. She sat up and blinked into reality. Laken was across the table from her, climbing up into a chair, a box of Cheerios already tipped over in front of her.

Alarmed, Brin checked the clock on the oven but discovered the power had gone out at some point. She glanced down at her wrist but realized she didn't have on her watch. She must've fallen asleep when she took a coffee break.

"What time is it?" she asked as she rose to peek out the window. The sun was coming up over the horizon and the skies appeared clear. She looked up at the ceiling and was relieved to see that the leaking had stopped and that the floor remained dry from her hours of mopping.

"Thank God the rain stopped," she said as she busied herself filling Laken's sippy cup with milk. Thankfully, the fridge was still cold and she hoped the power would be back on soon. She placed the cup on the table just as Laken was digging in on her handfuls of Cheerios. Brin knew she should try out the spoon at some point, but Tara had told her not to rush things, and today would be one heck of a day to try. Her house was literally falling down around her. The use of a spoon would have to wait until another day.

Laken drank her milk and ate, and Brin made herself some coffee. She sat and watched Laken and stared out at the rising sun. She had a problem on her hands. A big problem. And his name was Jimmy Roberts. What was she going to do? The guy obviously didn't have a clue how to fix things, and yet he seemed so self-assured and determined.

How could someone be that confident and yet clueless?

Did he just not care?

And how could Miley keep talking him up? Was she that clueless as well?

At the moment, she felt like she was the most clueless one of them all. After all, Corey had warned her. But she'd thought, what? It was some sort of jealousy thing? A territorial thing?

Why had she thought that? Was it because of the way Jimmy had been acting? And she'd somehow blamed Corey for it and put it on her?

God, I don't know.

She sank her head down into her hands. The smell of chewed Cheerios was making her sick. She sipped her coffee and prayed it would settle her nervous stomach. But honestly, she knew nothing was going to do the trick. So when Laken finished eating, she got her dressed and took her out front to examine the fallen tree.

Laken held her hand as their breath showed itself in white puffs. They stood at the tree in silence, with the bright morning sun stinging their eyes.

Eventually, Laken dropped her hand and pointed at the fallen trunk.

"It fell, didn't it?" Brin said.

Laken stepped closer and began picking at the dead bark, peeling the tree as if the bark were dry skin needing to come off. She seemed fascinated so Brin allowed it. She again looked to the house and thanked her lucky stars the damn tree hadn't fallen the other way. It would have crashed into her kitchen for sure. And inches the other way and it would have demolished her car. All in all, they really were extremely lucky.

"The good news is that it didn't fall on the house or the car," she said to Laken. "But the bad news is we still have one heck of a leak." She glanced up at the roof, wondering if she could see the damage from where she stood. She couldn't.

"And the town Bozo is convinced he's the one to fix it," she said under her breath.

Just then she heard a vehicle approaching. She cringed, hoping it wasn't Jimmy. She wasn't quite in the mood for him yet. She turned and saw Corey's truck headed up the road. The old engine was loud and it sputtered as it drew closer.

"Great."

She watched Corey approach, hoping maybe a quick wave would suffice, but to her dismay, Corey slowed and pulled in the driveway.

The last thing Brin needed was a lecture, but she was sure that's what she was about to get.

Corey killed her noisy engine and crawled from the truck. She adjusted her ball cap as she walked up to Brin.

"Morning."

"Good morning."

God, she looks good even first thing in the morning. Who knew that jeans and a fleece pullover could do it for me?

Corey held her gaze a moment, seemingly oblivious to her thoughts before her eyes slid over to the downed tree. Brin braced herself for the onslaught of "I told you sos." But Corey merely bypassed her in silence and walked up to Laken, who was still busy playing with the bark.

"Hey, Laken. Whatcha doin'?" She knelt and examined the bark and then straightened. "She's got quite a collection going there."

Brin shrugged. "She's amused, so I'm letting her play."

"No harm in that," Corey said as she came back to stand near Brin.

They stood in silence for a while before Brin spoke up, unable to take it.

"I suppose you're going to lecture me now. About the tree."

Corey stared off into the distance. Brin could smell the soap from her shower and it set her body afire.

"Wouldn't dream of it," Corey said, again thankfully oblivious to Brin's near-drooling.

"What? Of course you would. I know you're just dying to."

Corey finally looked at her. "I'm just glad you're okay."

Brin clamped her mouth shut. She was shocked at her soft sincerity, and she blinked at her, unsure if she'd heard her correctly.

She had.

Brin glanced away, too moved to speak, too emotional to hold her gaze.

"Hey, what's wrong?" Corey asked, placing a gentle hand on her shoulder.

"Everything," Brin said. "The tree, the house…"

Corey frowned. "Don't tell me."

Brin nodded. "Yeah."

"How bad?"

Brin sighed. "Come on in and I'll show you."

CHAPTER SIXTEEN

"Oh, boy," Corey said as she inspected the damaged ceiling. She removed her hat and scratched her head. "What in the hell did he do up there?"

"I'm not sure," Brin said. "He just kept telling me he took care of everything and not to worry."

Corey surveyed the floor. "And water was where?"

"Everywhere."

Corey shook her head. "Well, I'll have to get my ladder and go take a look to see what all he did or didn't do." She paused and tapped her hat against her thigh. "If that's okay with you?"

Brin laughed. "Yes, that's more than okay with me. And I'm sorry I didn't listen when you tried to warn me."

Corey waved her off. "No worries. We're good."

"Are we? I mean, are you sure?"

Corey leaned on the counter. She didn't like the look of concern on Brin's face. "I know how pushy those two can be."

"I just thought…well, he kept insisting that he could fix it. I mean, who does that unless they really know how, you know?"

Corey chuckled. "Jimmy Roberts that's who. I guess I don't have to tell you to never buy a used car off of him, do I?"

"No. Geez. I can't imagine. How does he stay in business?"

"Beats me."

Corey pushed away from the counter as Laken came bounding in the room carrying two small squash. She held one up for Corey.

"Hey, thanks, kiddo."

Laken ran back out of the room.

Brin shook her head. "She only ever does that with you."

Corey smiled. She set the squash on the counter and placed her hat back on her head. "I better go see about that ladder."

Brin followed her to the door. "I really appreciate it, Corey."

"No problem whatsoever." She faced Brin once again. "I just want to make sure you two are safe."

Brin returned the smile but visibly flushed. "Thanks."

Corey tugged on the brim of her hat and walked out to her truck. She climbed inside and headed back to her ranch for the ladder and supplies. It seemed she was going to be able to use the goods she'd bought from Flick after all.

Half an hour later, she was back at Brin's and climbing up the side of her house. It didn't take her anytime at all to figure out where Jimmy had gone wrong. The fool didn't fix the underlayment or seal any of it properly.

How anyone who claimed he could fix a roof could do this was beyond her. She rubbed the back of her neck as she examined the damaged area. Then she walked the length of the house and found two more areas that would soon be problems if they weren't taken care of.

Had he not seen these?

Just how big of an idiot was he?

She climbed back down and knocked on Brin's door.

Brin opened it but she held a finger up. She was on the phone.

"No, I don't need you to come by. Really, I'm fine. I'm—" She held the phone away from her ear and looked at it. Then she looked at Corey.

"He hung up on me."

"Who?"

"Jimmy!"

Corey laughed. "Always Mr. Manners."

Brin sighed and tossed the phone on the couch before sinking down into the cushions. Laken sat on the floor, positioning small toy dinosaurs. She had a whole line of them heading into the hallway.

Brin, seeing Corey's interest, nodded toward Laken. "She'll have them leading into every room in the house."

"That explains the toy bin full of them," Corey said, watching as Laken dug through the collection to find the one she wanted next.

"What can I say? She loves them and I tend to give in."

"Understandable," Corey said, still watching in amazement. Laken's ability to focus and concentrate on the task at hand was really quite impressive. She envied her.

"Would you prefer to help her rather than work on the roof?" Brin asked.

Corey chuckled. "Don't tempt me."

"I wouldn't blame you." She paused. "What exactly is wrong with the roof? Do I want to know?"

Corey motioned toward the armchair across from Brin.

"Please," Brin said.

Corey sat. "He—Good Lord, he screwed up the whole thing. He messed up the underlayment, didn't seal anything properly—"

Brin held up her hand to stop her. "That's bad, isn't it?"

"Yes, that's bad."

"Can it be fixed?"

"It'll have to be redone, and I'll need more supplies from Flick, but yes."

"How much is that going to set me back?"

Corey rested her elbows on her knees. "Brin, you have to have a roof."

"Yes. I know this."

"So, why don't you just let me fix it and we'll worry about all that later?"

"But you need supplies, don't you?"

"I've already got some of them. They're in the back of my truck."

Brin straightened her back. "Oh."

Corey allowed the information to sink in. Then she spoke softly. "So, what do you say? You gonna let me help you out?"

Brin stared at the floor.

"Before you answer…have you ever considered the fact that Jimmy might be screwing things up on purpose?"

"On purpose?"

"To, you know, have to keep coming around?"

Brin's eyes widened. "Oh, God."

"Uh-huh. The way he messed up that roof, the shoddy job he did, it didn't even make sense."

"So, you think he's doing things on purpose?"

"I've known Jimmy a long time and I wouldn't put it past him. And if I were you, I'd not only fire him, I'd refuse to pay him."

"Okay, but if I go with you, you have to let me help pay you somehow. I don't like owing people."

"I understand." She glanced at Laken and then looked back to Brin. She looked so beautiful in the golden morning light. Her hair was lit up like a halo and her eyes were burning with intensity. At that moment Corey realized she'd do anything for her. Anything for her and Laken. It was a realization that startled her, as she'd only known them for a short amount of time. And the last time she cared this much for someone, they'd run off and emptied her bank account and spent it all on painkillers.

The memory left a bad taste in her mouth, and it caused her to want to create new ones. She had to believe in herself and her own convictions. Not every woman was like Dawn so maybe it was time to prove it.

Corey cleared her throat. "How about dinner? I fix the roof and you cook?"

"Dinner? That's it? That's all you want?"

"You *can* cook, can't you?" Corey lifted the corner of her mouth in a playful smile.

Brin returned it. "It's been a while since I've made anything other than Cheerios and chicken nuggets, but yes."

"Then yes, dinner it is."

"You're sure?"

"Uh-huh. But of course you should know that you have two more areas on your roof that need tending to, so it's going to need to be more than one dinner."

"Ah, I see."

"You good with that?"

"As long as you let me pay you actual money at some point."

Corey raised an eyebrow. "You're going to insist on that, aren't you?"

"'Fraid so."

Corey sighed. "Alright then. But I don't want you to worry about it. Not right now anyway." She stuck out her hand. "Deal?"

Brin smirked and took her hand. It was soft and incredibly warm, and Corey didn't want to let go. And for the briefest of seconds she saw something in Brin's eyes that suggested she felt the same.

"Deal," Brin said.

"Good, I'll go get started." Corey released her hand and stood. Brin rose with her.

"You're starting right now?"

"No time like the present."

She cocked her head. "Funny. That's what I always say."

"Well, then, you won't stop me."

"No, I won't stop you."

"Good, because we're in for a wet winter and another storm is likely on the way."

She opened the front door to see that Ryan was pulling in with his pickup truck. She looked back to Brin. "My help has just arrived."

Brin smiled. "Glad to know you aren't trying to do this alone."

"I'm proud not stupid."

Brin laughed. But her laughter faltered as another vehicle pulled in the driveway. Corey squinted for a better look.

"Is that Miley?"

Brin grumbled. "Looks like it."

"I'll be on the roof if you need me."

"Thanks," Brin huffed.

"Hey, if you want me to handle her, I will."

"No, you go on. I got this. I think."

Corey studied her for a moment longer and then walked out the door. She met Miley at the base of the porch steps.

"Well, good morning, Corey. Imagine finding you here." She flashed her long lashes and smiled her biggest, fakest, put-upon smile. Corey was so used to it she'd even perfected one to give in return.

"Well, good morning, Miley. I'm somewhat surprised to see you here, too. And with what? A casserole?" She eyed the dish in Miley's hands.

"It's a breakfast casserole. Made it up special for Brin and little Larkin."

Corey laughed under her breath. "It's Laken. Not Larkin."

But Miley ignored her and continued unperturbed.

"I'm afraid there might not be enough for you and your friend. Not after Brin gets a taste, and of course, Jimmy and myself."

"So you're staying for breakfast, then?"

"Of course."

"Does Brin know this?"

"She will soon enough. Soon as she sees all the trouble I went to I just know she'll insist." She started to walk away but stopped. "Ya'll aren't planning on doing anything to that roof, are you?"

"Matter of fact, we are."

"Well, Jimmy's coming to fix it."

"Jimmy's done enough fixing."

Miley frowned and Corey left her in her wake. She met Ryan at his truck and followed his line of sight back to the house where Brin had answered the door. She couldn't hear what they were saying, but she could tell by the look on Brin's face that she wasn't happy. Wasn't happy at all.

"She worming her way in again?" Ryan asked.

"She's trying."

"What a crazy lady," he said.

"The worst is yet to come," Corey said, reaching in the back of her truck to strap on her tool belt.

"How's that?"

"Jimmy's on his way over."

"They're gonna tag team her."

"Not if I can help it."

"What did he do to this roof, anyhow?"

Corey grinned. "You're not gonna believe it till you see it."

"Worse than my first roofing repair?"

"Oh, kid. It puts yours to shame."

Corey helped him secure his belt and then patted him on the shoulder. "You go on up first."

She and Ryan got busy hoisting the supplies up onto the roof. She'd almost forgotten about Jimmy until he pulled into the driveway, gravel flying everywhere, rear end fishtailing as he braked. She had to give it to him. The man did know how to make an entrance.

She stood next to Ryan on the roof as Jimmy threw open his door and climbed out, his gaze already fixed on the two of them.

He wagged a finger at them and spittle flew from his mouth as he spoke.

"What do you think you're doing, Corey Durand?"

Corey held her arms out to her sides. "We're fixing a roof, Jimmy Roberts. What do you think you're doing?"

He rushed toward them, finger still wagging. "You can't do that. You just can't do that. This here is my job. I'm fixing the roof."

Corey placed her hands on her hips. "That's not the case anymore, Jimmy. Plans have changed."

"Says who? You?" He grinned wickedly. "I know what you're up to. You're trying to get in good with her, aren't you? So you can get with her."

Corey clenched her jaw, offended at his brashness. "No, Jimmy, she just wants a roof that doesn't leak."

"I know! I'll fix it. Just—get down from there!"

Corey heard the front door open and Miley and Brin came outside with Laken running behind. As soon as Laken saw Corey and Ryan on the roof, she made a beeline for the ladder.

Brin darted after her while Jimmy continued his rant, this time speaking to his sister.

"Laken!" Brin scooped her up and carried her away from the ladder. She started to cry and kick her feet. "You can't, love. It's dangerous."

Corey felt helpless watching the unfolding fiasco from afar.

"Hold down the fort, kid. I'll be right back." She left Ryan and descended the ladder, wondering just what all awaited her at the bottom.

CHAPTER SEVENTEEN

Brin hurried back toward the house with Laken in her arms, kicking and screaming. She heard Jimmy yelling in the background and Miley calling her name as she put in her two cents, but honestly, Brin couldn't make out what they were saying. The only thing she cared about was getting Laken inside where it was safe.

She reached the front door and set her down, keeping a strong grip on her hand. She yelled at Jimmy and Miley.

"If you two want to talk to me you better come inside now. I'm going to have to lock the doors once I'm inside."

She wished like hell they'd just leave, but she knew they wouldn't. They'd bang on the door like imbeciles, insisting on speaking to her.

And she was right. They immediately stopped their tirade and followed her into the house.

"I can't believe that Corey Durand," Miley said. "I told you to get here sooner!" She slugged Jimmy in the arm.

"I came as quick as I could. I can't help that she lives next door."

Brin bolted the door with the child safety lock and then did the same to the back door. She lifted Laken back into her arms and sat with her on the couch, handing her her tiny squash, hoping they'd be a distraction. To her surprise, she found that Laken did stop crying, but only to focus on Jimmy and Miley who were still going at it like schoolchildren.

"You know why she's doing it," Jimmy said. "To get to her. You know, to—"

"Hey, hey!" Brin said, unwilling to listen to Jimmy accuse Corey of anything.

The nerve of this guy.

"Enough!"

Jimmy and Miley fell silent. But neither of them sat. Miley stood and stared while Jimmy paced like a caged animal, with quick glances out the window as if he could somehow see what Corey and Ryan were up to. The absurdity of it almost made Brin laugh.

But then Jimmy turned away from the window, eyes wide. "She's coming."

Miley scoffed. "Good. I want to give her a piece of my mind."

Brin gently set Laken aside and rose to answer the door. She rebolted it after Corey stepped inside.

Corey gave her a reassuring look and placed a soft hand on her shoulder. Brin wanted to melt beneath its strength, but she didn't dare in front of Miley Roberts, who was already studying them closely.

Corey seemed to notice her close scrutiny as well and she nodded a polite hello. "Miley. Jimmy."

"Corey," Miley said as her gaze traveled up and down Corey disapprovingly. Brin wondered what she thought of her in comparison. She, like Corey, was dressed casually in jeans. The only difference was that she was wearing a mauve sweater rather than a fleece pullover. So, why was Miley giving Corey an obviously disapproving once-over when she hadn't given her one?

"We were just having a private discussion," Miley said. "With Brin."

"If it concerns the roof, then I think I had better be included," Corey said.

"It does, but there's no need for your input," Jimmy said. "Like I said, I've got it."

"No, you don't. Not anymore," Corey said. She flexed her jaw as she fixed her eyes on him. Brin had never seen her so intense.

"Says who?"

"Says me."

Jimmy laughed. "You? How about we ask Brin?"

"Fine."

They all three looked to Brin, who stood feeling very awkward and exposed.

"Brin, who do you want to fix the roof?" Miley asked with a smile, holding her casserole out and proud. "I'm sure Jimmy knows exactly what went wrong and he can fix it in no time."

"No time at all," Jimmy said.

Corey grunted. "You're dressed for the car lot, not fixing a roof."

"I'm going to go home and change."

"No need," Corey said. "Right, Brin?"

Brin swallowed. "Right."

Miley's body softened in obvious defeat, but she held her smile. "But Jimmy's the one who's been working on it. He knows exactly what to do."

Brin felt her cheeks heat. "I think it's time someone else take over. I had water all over my kitchen floor, and I just really need it taken care of—"

"The *right* way," Corey said.

"And who's to do that?" Miley asked. "You, Corey Durand?"

"Yes."

She looked back to Brin. "Surely you can see what's happening here."

"What's that?" Corey asked.

"Well, it's obvious. You're trying to win her over."

Corey laughed and Brin burned hotter at the suggestion.

Miley however, continued. "Brin, sweetie, don't let her fool you. She's moving in on you. To—I don't know, seduce you."

"She's gay. You know how they operate," Jimmy said.

Corey took a step toward him, obviously fuming.

Brin held up a hand, totally and completely offended herself.

"Enough!"

All eyes were fixed on her once again.

"I want Corey to repair the roof. Jimmy, you and Miley can go."

Jimmy and Miley stared at her incredulously.

"But—" Jimmy started.

Miley's plastic-looking smile broadened. "You heard the woman, Jimmy. We're no longer welcome."

"I didn't say that," Brin said.

Wait, maybe I did.

"Seems we're already too late," Miley continued, turning toward the door. "Let's leave the two ladies alone. Like they *want.*"

Brin stood stuck to the floor as Corey rushed to the door and opened it for them. Miley set her casserole on an end table.

"Might as well enjoy it. I made it especially for you. And I'm not one to go back on my word."

It was a jab that hit Brin hard and she nearly faltered. She wanted to say something more, anything more, but nothing came. Corey, seeming to sense her shock and discomfort, quickly closed the door and locked it. Then she looked out the window after them.

"Are they gone?" Brin asked, hugging herself, feeling as if she'd been chilled to the bone.

"Not quite. They're still looking back at the house."

"I wish they'd just go."

"They will. They are. There. They're going." She faced Brin once again. "They're gone."

"Thank God."

"Are you okay?"

Brin rubbed her arms, the chill not yet subsiding. "I'm not sure."

"Don't let her get to you."

"I'm afraid she did."

"Well, I would tell you that she's just plain ol' full of shit and not to worry about it, but I'd be deceiving you."

"What do you mean?"

"I mean that the stance you just took could very well give you cause for worry."

"Why is that?"

"Because Miley is going to tell everyone you chose me over Jimmy because you and I are together."

"What? I know she implied it, but come on. She's not serious."

"Oh, she's serious alright. Jimmy even implied the same thing to me outside."

"They think we're together?"

"Or headed that way. That somehow I'm going to seduce you by fixing your roof."

Brin laughed but her blush deepened. Could Miley really see into her so well? Knowing that she would indeed fall for that mere suggested seduction? Or was it just a homophobic paranoia on her part, used as an excuse as to why she was rejecting her brother?

It didn't seem to matter. If what Corey said was true, the whole town was going to hear of it and make up their own minds. And that…that could be trouble.

She eyed her laptop and thought of her livelihood. Thought of the small town in which she'd just moved.

That….could indeed be a problem.

"But we aren't doing anything."

"I don't think she cares," Corey said.

"Corey, I—"

Brin eased onto the couch. Laken held out a squash for her. She took it but kept her focus on Corey.

"I—that wouldn't be very good for me."

"What wouldn't? The rumor of you and I together?" She looked concerned, almost…hurt.

Brin shook her head. "My sexuality. I didn't plan on telling anyone. I just wanted to move here with a fresh start for Laken and me. And put all my focus on her."

Corey blinked at her. "You don't want anyone to know you're gay?"

"Not really, no."

"Why?"

Brin rubbed her forehead. "I just don't, okay?" She had a livelihood to protect. She couldn't go through what she had in the past. Especially when that livelihood was literally all she had. She didn't have another income to fall back on. And now knowing what a gossip hound Miley Roberts was, she felt threatened.

"Then why did you tell me?"

Brin shot her a look. "Because I trust you."

Corey glanced away from her and crossed her arms over her chest.

"I can, can't I?" Brin asked, disliking her sudden avoidance in eye contact. "Trust you?"

Corey stared out the window. "Of course you can. It's just that…I may have told Grey."

"Told Grey what? That I'm gay?"

"Yes."

"Great."

"Well, I didn't know it was some big secret."

"Even so…"

"I'm sorry," Corey said.

"Why was that even a topic of conversation?" What had they been talking about? And why?

"I don't know," Corey said, but she still wouldn't look at her.

Brin didn't push it. She surmised she wasn't ready for the answer, regardless of what it was. Right now she was worried about Miley and Jimmy and their intentions.

"I've pissed off the wrong people, haven't I?"

Corey didn't respond.

"I thought as much."

"I'll—I don't know. Try to talk to her," Corey said, finally turning to look at her.

"Good luck with that," Brin said, already knowing it would be useless. "If anything you'll only fuel her fire even more."

"Yeah, well, I'll take my chances."

"You don't have to."

"No, I do. I feel bad about it. With what it could mean for you. I didn't know you were so private."

Brin stroked Laken's hair. She was nodding off sitting up so she brought her closer and snuggled her. All the drama had obviously gotten to her. She always slept after an emotional episode.

"Doesn't matter," Brin said softly. "What happens happens."

"No, it does matter. I don't like my business spread all over this town either. But…"

"But what?"

"You should know. Some people have already begun talking."

"About me?"

"About us."

"What are they saying?"

"That I'm interested in you."

"Are you serious? Why would they say that?"

Are you interested in me, Corey Durand? Is there something behind all this rumor and suggestion?

Corey shrugged. "Maybe because they saw us together at Miley's party or at the pumpkin patch or in town. And well, I'm gay. Therefore I'll go after any available woman around. You know how us gays are."

"We are quite the sex-starved vampires, aren't we? Good heavens. Have people got nothing better to do?"

"Apparently not."

"Then I guess we're in for a whole heap of trouble with you fixing my roof."

Corey sank her hands into her back pockets. "You gotta have a roof."

Brin pulled Laken closer and kissed the top of her head. "That I do."

Corey watched them for a moment with a soft expression on her face. Then she turned and unlatched the door.

"Guess I better get back to it."

"Guess so."

She stepped outside and Brin called after her, suddenly moved by her kind and giving nature.

"Hey, Durand?"

Corey turned. "Yeah?"

"What do you want for dinner?"

Corey smiled. "Surprise me."

CHAPTER EIGHTEEN

"A little more," Corey yelled as she guided Ryan in his truck. He gave the newer Ford some gas and the tree cracked as it broke completely and slid along the ground, kicking up gravel as it did so.

"Good, now a little more and then turn," Corey called out. Ryan waved at her and watched in his side mirror as he steered the tree off to the side of the driveway. Corey continued to guide him until the dead tree was free and clear.

Ryan climbed from his truck and they untied the tree from the tow ropes.

"What now?" he asked as they worked.

Corey wiped the sweat from her brow and replaced her hat on her head.

"We cut it up and use it as firewood."

"Cool. Does that mean I get to use the chainsaw?"

"If you help me finish up that last repair on the roof it does."

He smirked. "'Bout time. You've been the one getting all the reward for *our* hard work."

Corey chuckled. "Yep, and it's been so good, too."

"I don't understand. Does Brin not like me?"

Corey laughed harder. "Of course she does. But the deal was made between us. Not you."

"Still, some leftovers would be nice."

"She's sent some for you, you know."

"She has?"

"Uh-huh. I've just eaten them is all." She grinned and he smacked her on the arm.

"I knew it! I knew Brin wouldn't leave me hanging like that. Dang you, Corey."

Corey rubbed her arm. "I'll make it up to you, I promise. In the meantime you get to use the chainsaw."

"Tomorrow?"

She nodded.

"Right on."

She stared into the waning sun. "Good work today."

"Thanks."

"No, thank you, kid. You're doing great."

He smiled bashfully and kicked the gravel.

"Guess I'll go on back to the ranch now and do my evening stable chores while you go have a nice dinner."

"Don't forget to check on the goats for me. Wiley's been getting out of the pen."

"Will do. Night, boss."

"Night, kid."

She waved good-bye and headed for the front door. It opened as she walked up the porch steps and Laken came bounding out holding up dinosaurs.

"Heya, kiddo," Corey said. "Thank you so much." She took the offered dinosaurs and the two of them walked inside. Corey could already smell the meal cooking and her stomach rumbled a little.

"Come on in," she heard Brin call as she headed back to the kitchen. "It's almost ready."

"Smells great."

"I hope it tastes great."

"I'm sure it will."

She walked through the living room, noting how nice it looked compared to the first day she'd seen it. Brin had finished painting and had replaced the base boards. The vintage wood floor still needed refinishing, but it had been polished and it shined beneath her feet. A new-looking off-white shag rug covered most of it. That was where Laken had settled down to play with her dinosaurs. She was already back to intently concentrating on them.

Corey also noticed that Brin had covered the older armchair and couch with matching pale yellow slipcovers and accompanying throw pillows that gave the room a fresh, shabby chic motif. She'd even painted the old coffee table an antique white to match the walls. Framed photos of Laken hung near the fireplace, along with photos of a woman Corey assumed to be Laken's mother. The photos were tasteful and beautifully shot, and she wondered if they were professional or if Brin had a hidden talent for photography. All in all, the place looked much better. It was even beginning to have a homey feel to it.

Corey entered the kitchen where the smell of dinner was overwhelmingly welcome.

"The house sure is coming along," Corey said. "Living room looks great."

"Thanks," Brin said, placing silverware on the table. "As of today, it's my one and only finished room."

"You did a lot in a day."

"It helps having Laken go to therapy and daycare. Frees up some time to do the things around here that need to be done."

"It's getting there," Corey said. "And it's looking good."

Brin smiled at her. "Thanks."

"Is there anything I can do to help with dinner?"

"Drinks," Brin said, handing her a glass. "Help yourself. I also have bottles of beer in the fridge if you prefer those."

"Thanks, I think I'll take one if you don't mind."

"Not at all," Brin said. "Grab me one too, will you? Might as well share the joy."

Corey set down the glass and retrieved two bottles of beer from the fridge while Brin poured juice into a child's cup for Laken.

Corey set Brin's bottle on the table and then opened her own. She looked up at the ceiling where she and Ryan had done their recent repairs.

"The ceiling looks good. If I do say so myself."

Brin smiled and Corey tried not to stare at her in her tight white sweater and snug-fitting jeans. Her blond hair fell upon her shoulders in thick waves and Corey had to glance away so as not to imagine running her hands through it.

Laken ran into the kitchen just then with a large pair of headphones on. She climbed up in her chair and took a sip of juice from her cup. Then she sat and waited patiently for dinner. It seemed she no longer needed her booster seat.

"Wow," Corey said, smiling at her. "Such nice manners."

Brin returned the smile. "Oh, you wouldn't believe how far she's come since starting therapy with Tara. I can't thank you enough."

"I'm glad it's working out."

Brin motioned for her to join them at the table and Corey sat next to Laken and across from Brin.

"So, what's for dinner?"

"Slow cooker pot roast and mashed potatoes."

"Mm, sounds wonderful. Wish I woulda gone home to clean up. But I figured you've already seen me dirty, so…"

Corey held out her plate as Brin served her from a large serving dish.

"We like you dirty," Brin said. "It means you've been busy helping us out. Gravy?"

"Please."

She poured some gravy over her mashed potatoes and roast. Then she served herself and Laken.

"I'm not sure Laken will eat this. But what I am sure of, is that she'll try anything now. And…as of yesterday, she's trying out the spoon."

"That's great."

"It is." She forked a bite of roast and looked at Laken. "Laken, take a bite of roast for me, okay?"

Laken looked up and nodded. She scooped some roast and potatoes on her spoon and took a bite. She moved the food around in her mouth for a few seconds and then chewed and swallowed. Then she scooped another bite and did the same.

Brin chuckled. "Looks like it's a hit."

Corey took her own bite and groaned. "Mm, it sure is. It's really good."

"Do you not cook much?" Brin asked.

"Me? Nah. Every once in a while, Grey will have me over for a home cooked meal, but other than that it's mostly microwave dinners for me."

"You and Grey are good friends, aren't you?"

"She's my best friend. Known her for years."

"Yeah, you two seem tight."

"How about you?"

Brin's smile faded. "My sister was my best friend."

"Oh, I'm sorry."

"No, it's okay. It's just, times like these I really miss her. With the holidays coming up and all."

"I understand."

"And with how far Laken's coming along. I just really wish she could see it."

"I'm sure she can see it." Corey offered her a soft smile.

They sat in silence for a moment before Brin spoke again.

"Thanks for moving the tree," she said.

Corey nodded and swallowed. "It's out of the way for now. Tomorrow we'll start cutting it up so you can use it for firewood."

"Gosh, thanks, Corey. You don't have to go to all that trouble."

"It's no big deal. And I've noticed you've got zilch as far as firewood."

Brin sipped from her beer. "That's true."

"You'll be wanting that fireplace."

"I already do. I just have to get someone out here to sweep the chimney."

"I can do it."

"No, you've done enough already."

"Let me correct myself," Corey said. "Ryan can do it."

Brin laughed. "I'm sure he'd be thrilled at you volunteering him."

"He would be. The kid really likes you. And he…he has a heart of gold. Loves to help out."

"You two seem really close as well," Brin said.

Corey took a swig of beer. "He lost his father when he was young, and I sort of took on the mentor thing. He was boarding his horse at the ranch and he started hanging around more and more. So I took him under my wing. I've been looking out for him ever since."

"He's a nice young man."

Corey forked another bite. "He is. Got himself a girlfriend now, too."

"Get out. Really? Good for him."

"She's cute. The two of them are cute."

There was another noticeable silence.

"What about you? Why don't you have someone special?" Brin asked.

Corey took another bite to give herself time to think. How much was she willing to share? Seeing as how she still knew very little about Brin's life and past relationships, she decided to keep her cards close to her vest.

"I haven't had anyone in a while, and with as busy as I am, I just don't give women much thought."

Until recently.

"I find that hard to believe," Brin said. "That it's been a while."

"Well, it has."

Brin swallowed another bite. "Do you mind if I ask what happened? With your last relationship?"

Corey studied her. "You've heard some things?"

Brin half-shrugged. "Here and there."

Corey shoved her food around with her fork. She didn't usually want to get into the details, but Brin was asking politely and she was looking at her with such kindness and understanding, Corey felt her long erected walls begin to crumble slightly.

"I don't mean to pry," Brin said softly. "I'm just...curious about you."

"No, you're fine. I—" Corey took a deep breath. "I was with someone for many years. Her name was Dawn and we had a good life. But then she was in a bad car accident..."

"Oh, I'm so sorry," Brin said, looking devastated. "I didn't know or I wouldn't have brought it up."

"No, no," Corey said quickly. "She's fine. I mean she's alive. It's just that...Ah hell, she's not fine. She's not fine at all."

Corey set down her fork. Brin waited quietly.

"After the accident, she started taking painkillers and she got hooked."

"Oh, no."

"Yeah. And it got bad. Now she's…Christ…she does whatever she has to to get her opioid fix."

"I'm so sorry," Brin said.

"She steals. Lies. Whatever it takes."

"That must be so hard."

"It was," Corey said. "But I've let it all go. Let her go. I had to," she croaked.

Corey sipped her beer to help loosen her tightening throat.

"You still care about her," Brin said.

Corey shook her head. "No, I—"

"It's okay."

"I can't. You don't understand."

"I do."

Brin reached across the table and covered her hand. Corey inhaled at the warm contact and Brin squeezed.

"It's okay to care."

Corey fought tears. "I can't."

"But you do."

Corey looked away, too close to crying to hold her empathetic gaze.

"I just don't want anything bad to happen to her."

"Of course not."

"But I had to let her go."

"Yes, you did. And it sounds like you did nothing wrong in doing so."

Corey pushed out a shaky breath. "It feels like I did sometimes."

Brin squeezed her hand again. "No."

They sat in silence. Laken continued to eat and listen to her music.

"Does she, do you still see her?"

"No. She doesn't come around. And if she did…I don't know. It would be hard."

"Do you still love her?"

Corey nearly choked. She met her penetrating gaze and knew for certain how to answer.

But she couldn't voice it. Her tight throat wouldn't let her. Brin patted her hand and released her.

"Of course you do," she said.

"No," Corey rasped.

"I understand. You were together a long time." She began clearing the table. "Love like that must be difficult to let go."

Corey rose and began helping her. "But I don't."

"It's okay, Corey. You don't have to defend yourself or explain yourself to me."

"But—"

"Let's just forget it, okay?"

She was moving quickly, her movements short and sharp. She was obviously upset, but Corey was at a loss as to what to do. She was also at a loss as to why. Why did Brin care whether or not she still loved Dawn? Hell, Brin didn't want anyone to even know she was gay. So it couldn't be because she was interested.

"Forgotten," Corey said, as she stepped up next to her to help her wash the dishes.

Forgotten.

CHAPTER NINETEEN

Brin pulled in at the market and switched off her engine. She grabbed her purse and exited the car. The November air had a crispness to it that she was coming to enjoy. The mild winters in Phoenix seemed eons ago and she walked up to the automatic doors with a smile.

She'd just finished up some work at home and she was looking forward to picking up something for dinner for her last arranged meal with Corey. She had no idea what to make, but she wanted it to be special. Corey had done a lot for her and even though the revelation that she was probably still in love with her ex had stung, surprisingly so, she still wanted to show her how much she appreciated all her hard work.

She retrieved a shopping cart and began at the far aisle. She didn't need to buy much because she was going to Phoenix for Thanksgiving to visit her parents. It would be their first Thanksgiving without Breana and they really wanted to see her and Laken. Brin understood, though she would rather stay in Utopia and have a nice, quiet meal with Laken. The whole idea of her returning home and seeing the grief on her folks' faces didn't sound appealing. She was finally moving forward, in every aspect, and that included her grieving. She and Laken were doing wonderfully, and she didn't want anything to pop that bubble. Even if that needle might indeed be her parents.

Of course she also knew that if she stayed that Miley Roberts would probably get wind of it and insist on having them over to her place. Or who knows, she might even insist that she and Jimmy come back to theirs. At this point nothing would surprise Brin when it came to Miley and Jimmy.

Come to think of it, things had been rather quiet on that front. Since Corey had taken over on the roof, Miley and Jimmy both had been absent. They hadn't even called. She wondered if that was good or bad.

Probably bad.

She turned down the first aisle and wheeled her cart through the produce. A young man in a green apron nodded at her as he walked by. Another woman looked at her but didn't greet her. And yet another woman looked at her, did a double take, and then elbowed the women next to her, who also looked at her.

"Hello," Brin said, thinking maybe the treatment was just because she was the new girl in town.

The women mumbled hellos but then pushed their squeaky carts away from her.

"Real friendly," Brin said.

She picked out some bananas and continued her shopping. To her dismay, she got the same treatment from two other people.

Do I have something on my face?

She kept shopping and decided to keep to herself. She didn't risk saying hello to anyone else for fear of more stares and rejection. By the time she was ready to check out, she felt like she'd been walking through a mine field. Avoiding people as if they were live explosive devices ready to detonate at any second.

She wheeled her cart up to the checkout lane and began unloading her groceries.

"Hello," the cashier said.

"Hello," Brin said. The woman was young, maybe eighteen or so, with a broad smile and big hoop earrings. Her pink lipstick matched her eyeshadow and she had decorative pins covering the front of her smock. Her bright smile was a welcome sight.

"Find everything okay?" she asked.

"Yes, thank you."

"I haven't seen you in here before. Are you new in town?"

"I am," Brin said. "I'm Brin. I just moved here with my niece, Laken."

"Oh." The young woman straightened. "Then you must be buying groceries for another dinner with Corey Durand."

Brin blinked at her. "Sorry?"

But the young woman kept on, oblivious. "Corey's great. I really like her. She taught me how to ride my first horse. And when I was in fifth grade she sold my parents one of her goats. He was a feisty little thing. I named him Cujo even though he wasn't a dog. Made people think twice about messing with him though." She laughed as if she'd amused herself.

Brin just stood there, incredulous. "How did you know I was making dinner for Corey?"

The young woman shrugged. "I don't know. I just heard it around town. Corey's fixing your roof and you two are having dinner dates."

"Whoa, that's not what's happening."

"It's not?"

Brin stammered. "They aren't dates per se."

The young woman shrugged again. "Whatever. That'll be sixty-three fifty."

"No, really. We aren't dating. I'm just making her dinner to return the favor."

"Okay." She cocked her head as she took Brin's money. "It's really no big deal, you know. Most people don't care anymore."

"I—I'm sure they don't." But the way people had just reacted around her told of another story.

Brin took her change and deposited it quickly in her purse. "That's not the point."

"You ask me, it's time Corey moved on. And you seem nice enough."

Brin didn't have time to respond.

"Would you like any help out?"

"What? No. No, thank you." She grabbed her groceries and hurried outside. As she stepped up to her car and tried to open the trunk she nearly dropped a bag. Thankfully though, someone came to her rescue.

"I got it," the older man said, taking the falling bag from her. "Nice and easy." He helped her open the trunk and place the bags inside. Then he stuck out his hand.

"Name's Flick."

"Hi." Brin shook his hand and smiled. "Thank you, so much. I nearly dropped everything."

"Don't mention it. Sometimes we need more than two hands."

"You can say that again."

His blue eyes twinkled at her in the sun, and he placed his hand in the front pocket of his leather vest.

"Say, you're the new girl, aren't you?"

"Guilty as charged," she said. "Brin. I seem to be pretty popular today. I think everyone in the grocery store knew who I was even though I'd never seen them before in my life."

"Aw, don't let them get to you. We're all just curious small-town folk. Besides, you are pretty popular, you know? Especially now with you spending all that time with Corey Durand." He winked at her.

"Contrary to what the rumors are, it's not what everyone thinks."

His eyes widened a bit. "Well, that's too damn bad. I was hoping Corey had finally found some happiness. She deserves it. And you could do worse."

"I'm sure I could and I can assure you, it has nothing to do with Corey. I'm just—it's just not what everyone thinks."

"Hm." He rubbed his white scruffy jaw. "Guess I stand corrected then. As do most folk. Shoulda known it when I heard some of it coming from Miley Roberts."

Brin winced and he chuckled.

"Well, I better get back to my store. It was nice meeting you, new girl." He squeezed her upper arm. "You have yourself a good day, now. And don't let the rumor mill get you down."

"I'll try not to," she said as he walked away. "I'll try."

❖

"Something the matter?" Tara asked as Brin stood waiting by the front counter for Laken to finish up her therapy session.

Brin forced a smile and then gave up and threw up her hands. "Am I that obvious?"

"Little bit, yeah." Tara leaned on the counter. "Anything I can help with?"

"Let's just say I'm starting to regret moving to such a small town."

"Oh?"

"The gossip is just…"

"Oh, that. Yeah, it's pretty bad. Everybody's in everybody else's business. It gets old, fast."

"Yes, it does. I haven't even been in Utopia very long at all and I can't believe the rumors that are going around."

"About you?"

"Well, yes. Myself and another."

"You mean you and Corey?"

Brin felt her mouth fall open. "You, too?"

Tara laughed. "Uh-huh. I've heard from a friend of mine who lives in Utopia. Seems that you and Corey are hitting it off very well. Very well indeed."

Brin palmed her forehead. "Oh, my God. I don't believe it!"

"Believe it, woman. You two seem to be the talk of the town."

"But why?"

"From what I've heard it's because Corey's spending so much time with you."

"Yes, but she's fixing my roof! That's it. And I'm making her dinner as a thank you. How does that lead to us being—I don't know—"

"Hot and heavy?"

"Yes!"

"Could be the condoms Corey was seen in town buying."

"What?"

"Someone saw her buying condoms at the drugstore. Guess everyone assumes they're for use with you."

"Oh. My. God."

Tara laughed heartily. "Don't put anything past the imagination of small-town folk."

"I guess not."

"Personally, I wouldn't have jumped to that conclusion, but I would have wondered what the hell she was doing with them."

"I don't believe this. Now you've got me wondering."

Tara laughed again. "See? The gossip is infectious, isn't it?"

"Apparently so." She stared at Tara. "What *is* she doing with them?"

"Beats me."

"Well, if she's using a strap-on, it's not with me."

Tara cracked up. "I'll be sure to let everyone know."

"Please do. I don't like being at the center of this web of gossip."

Laken ran up to them just then and Tara knelt and gave her a high five. "You did great today, little one. Keep up the good work."

"Hi!" Brin said as she scooped her up. "What all did you do today?"

Laken pointed at the ball pit.

"Did you have fun?"

She nodded and then buried her face in Brin's shoulder.

"Did you see that?" Brin asked Tara.

"I did."

"Oh, my God, she answered me!"

"Yes, she did."

"Laken! You answered me!" Brin held her in her arms and swung her around causing Laken to giggle. "You just made my day, kiddo!" She kissed her face all over, causing more giggles.

"She's really doing very well," Tara said. "Today she ate some ravioli."

"You're kidding?"

"We just put the ravioli in her mouth and when she ate it we rewarded her with a Cheeto."

"Good ol' Cheetos. Gosh, I never thought she'd eat ravioli. I'm so glad," Brin said, adjusting her on her hip.

"She's come a long way in a short amount of time."

"Yes, she has. She seems so much happier, too."

"I think she is. Anyone would be coming out of their shell."

Brin smiled at Laken. "Wanna go home and make dinner for Corey?"

"Corey," Laken said softly.

Brin felt her eyes widen. "Yes, love, Corey!" She looked to Tara. "She spoke! Oh, my God, she spoke!"

Tara laughed. "Hold on tight, Aunt Brin. She's going to continue to surprise you from here on out."

"Wow, I guess so."

Brin bounced her and Laken wiped her eyes. "Okay, let's go before you pass out on me."

Tara stroked Laken's arm. "Bye, Laken. We'll see you soon."

"Bye," Brin said. "And thanks so much. For everything."

Tara nodded and waved as they walked out.

Brin stepped into the sunshine and walked with Laken hand in hand, her troubles and worries suddenly long behind her. Today, Laken answered her. Today, Laken spoke.

She glanced around, hoping to see someone she knew. For that was something she really wouldn't mind getting around.

CHAPTER TWENTY

Corey leaned on her rake as a vehicle she didn't recognize pulled alongside the pumpkin patch.

"Who in the world is that?" Grey asked, tugging on the brim of her cowboy hat.

"Not sure."

The sedan was older and had seen better days. One of the doors was a different color than the rest of the car, and rust lined the wheel wells. It stopped near the fence line and the driver sat for a moment, as if contemplating their next move.

Corey removed her gloves and tucked them in her back pocket as she made her way toward the mysterious vehicle. To be honest, she was thankful for a break. Cleaning up the pumpkin patch was hard work and they'd been at it for hours.

"I'll be right back," she said as she walked through the entrance to the patch.

Grey called something out after her as the driver climbed from the car, but Corey couldn't make it out. She waved at the stranger but then froze as the stranger rounded the vehicle and came into better view. Now she knew what Grey had said. She'd tried to warn her.

"Hi," Dawn said with a cautious smile.

Corey stood completely still. She was unable to move or to speak. It was almost like what she was seeing was a mirage, not real. But there she was, in the flesh, looking thinner than she'd ever seen her, with her hair long and stringy and her eyes sunken. She looked like a ghost of the woman she once was.

"I hope you don't mind my stopping by," she said, obviously still feeling uneasy.

Corey didn't comfort her any. She couldn't. Instead Grey came up behind her and spoke for her.

"What do you want, Dawn?"

"I came to talk to Corey," she said, her face hardening.

"Corey doesn't want to talk to you."

"Corey hasn't said that." Dawn met Corey's gaze. "Please. I just want a word."

Corey blinked back to reality. She had no idea what Dawn wanted, but if she took the chance in showing up to talk to her it must be important. She'd never be able to live with herself if it was something she could help with. Like what if she were sick and dying and Corey turned her away, refusing to listen.

No, she had to at least hear her out.

"Let's go inside," Corey said.

"You don't have to," Grey said, gently gripping her arm. "You don't owe her a damn thing."

"I know," Corey said softly.

Grey released her and Corey walked off toward the house with Whip by her side.

"Hey, Whip," Dawn said, whistling to him, but the dog paid her no mind, sticking right by Corey.

It seemed even the dog had learned his lesson in dealing with her.

Corey walked briskly, wanting to get whatever it was over with. When she entered the house, she stepped out of her boots and slid out of her coat. Then she made her way into the kitchen where she poured herself a strong shot of whiskey and downed it. Her heart was already careening in her chest and she needed it to slow. Needed everything to slow so she could focus and do and say what needed to be done and said.

But Dawn was hanging by the couch, tracing her fingertips along the arm, reminding Corey of how those fingertips once felt along her skin late at night.

"How can I—" Corey stopped herself. She wasn't about to ask her how she could help her. "What is it that you want?"

Dawn continued her maddening caress of the couch. "I heard you're seeing someone."

Corey nearly choked. "What?"

"It's all over town."

Corey shook her head. "Sorry, what is?"

"That you've got a new girlfriend."

"I do?"

"And I—I don't know. I thought maybe we could talk."

Corey wasn't following. Her head was awash with all things Dawn. Her scent, her laugh, her cries of pleasure.

Her promises.

"You did?"

"Uh-huh. I've been doing a lot of thinking and—"

"I'm sorry, who is my new girlfriend?"

Dawn sighed like she was annoyed. "I don't know. Some woman named Brin or something. Supposed to be your neighbor. Corey, don't play coy. I'm trying to be serious here."

Corey stood and stared. She thought about arguing about Brin, about telling her it wasn't true, but she wanted to play it safe. She wanted to see what Dawn would say if she thought the two of them were together.

"Go on."

"And, I don't know." She shrugged and gave a smile. "I just wanted to come tell you how much I still love you."

Heat flooded Corey's face as the words and the tilted grin registered. Her head swooned and her mind melted. She reached out, suddenly needing a place to regain her balance. She found a barstool and righted herself.

Dawn came closer as if she were concerned.

"Are you okay?"

"Fine," she rasped. But she wasn't. She was far from fine. For years now she'd dreamt of Dawn showing up and saying those exact words. But this was not how she envisioned herself reacting. She literally felt sick. As if the words were somehow poisonous and they'd infiltrated her bloodstream. She wanted to sit, needed to sit.

She stumbled onto the barstool and tossed her hat aside to bury her head in her hands. She trembled when she felt Dawn's hand on her shoulder.

"It's okay," she whispered. "It's all okay."

Corey forced herself to breathe deeply. "It's not," she said.

"It is, hon. It is. I love you and I want you back. I'm willing to fight for you if need be."

Corey laughed. She wasn't sure where it came from but it came. Loud and deep. She laughed so hard it hurt.

Just then the doorbell rang and Corey looked up. Who could that be?

But Dawn was already crossing to it. Corey hurriedly gave chase, but Dawn pulled the door open before she could reach it. And there stood Brin and little Laken with Brin holding out a covered dish.

Her angelic face fell as she caught sight of Dawn, but she still tried to sound friendly and nonchalant.

"We thought you might be hungry after working so hard on the pumpkin patch all day. So I brought you some of that casserole that you liked so well. But I've obviously come at a bad time." She handed Corey the dish and grabbed Laken's hand and turned to walk away.

Corey jerked to life as she realized what was happening. "Brin, no, don't go." She set the casserole aside and stepped outside after her.

"You have company. I should go."

"No, don't. It's just Dawn and she was just—"

"So this is the new girlfriend?" Dawn asked, causing both Brin and Corey to freeze.

Brin turned. "Excuse me?"

"It's a mistake," Corey stammered. "She heard it around town."

"People are saying I'm your girlfriend?"

"Yes. No. I'm not sure."

"What's wrong? Are you not her girlfriend?" Dawn asked, hands on hips.

"No, not that it's any of your business."

Dawn smiled. "Well, good, because we're getting back together."

Brin flinched ever so slightly, but Corey saw it. She saw it and she felt it.

And damn, did it sting.

"That's not true," Corey said as Brin started to move again.

"Come on, Laken. Let's leave these two lovebirds alone."

"No, Brin, wait. Let me explain."

"It doesn't matter, Corey," she said, meeting her gaze. "You can do as you please."

"But it's not true. She's—I don't know—crazy."

"Hey, I'm right here," Dawn said.

They reached Brin's car and Corey wanted so badly to press against the door to keep it closed, but she didn't. Instead she watched helplessly as Brin and Laken climbed in and buckled up. And then watched with her heart in her chest as the two of them drove away.

❖

Corey sat at the kitchen table and shoved the bottle of whiskey in front of her away. The last thing she needed was to get lost in alcohol. Then she'd be no better than Dawn, drowning her sorrows in a substance. She bowed her head and ran her fingers through her hair. She sighed as thunder boomed outside, shaking the house. A storm was now upon her, and it seemed to match the turmoil currently brewing inside her.

Dawn had left a couple of hours before. But not before causing all kinds of hell. She'd insisted she wanted Corey back and that she loved her and that she'd changed. But the track marks on her neck Corey had seen when she'd tried to hug her told of another story. She'd obviously moved on to injecting heroin to get her fix now, the painkillers probably too difficult to pay for or come by.

The sight had sickened Corey and she'd felt it then. Grief. Grief for the woman she'd lost. The lover she'd had to let go. She'd broken down and cried and Dawn had thought she'd won, trying to cradle her in her arms. But Corey had pushed her away and Grey had come in and run Dawn off and Corey had collapsed on the couch, crying.

Grey had tried to comfort her, but there was no comfort to be given. She'd needed to cry, to retch, to grieve. So Grey had given her her space and simply covered her up with a soft blanket and left. Corey had cried herself to sleep, finally free of the death she'd avoided facing for so long.

Now she felt tired and drained. The crying had left her limp and spent, like a wet noodle. She wanted nothing in the way of the whiskey or food. She just wanted…Brin.

It hit her then, much like how the revelation that she'd do anything for her had.

She wanted Brin.

She stood, ready to go to her, to take her in her arms and declare her feelings for her.

But she realized something. Something that made her stop in her tracks.

Brin didn't want her.

Brin didn't *want* her.

Brin didn't even want anyone to know she was gay, so how could she share her feelings with her and expect her to return them?

Lightning flashed and thunder cracked loudly overhead. Corey secured Whip's thunder jacket and watched as he went to his bed to settle beneath the blankets. Then she glanced out the window toward the back of the ranch, back beyond the pumpkin patch. Brin's house lit up in the darkness as another bout of thunder and lightning came.

And then it rained. Hard.

Corey, mind made up, hurried out the door. She didn't bother with a coat or hat, she just ran out to her truck and climbed in.

As she drove the short trek to Brin's, she tried to convince herself that she was only going to check on the house. She needed to make sure the new areas she'd patched up were holding. Brin was depending on it.

But even as she pulled into the driveway, she was less than convinced. So, she sat there for a few moments before going in, trying to pull herself together. She needed to be strong and confident. Someone Brin could trust and rely on. She couldn't be a blubbering mess.

After a few more moments, she climbed from her truck, knowing that at the very least she needed to explain what had happened with Dawn.

She walked slowly up to the door and knocked on the screen. The cold rain saturated her clothes and skin, but she didn't care.

Brin answered the door and a look of distress came over her.

"Corey. What are you—" She pulled the door open farther and held open the screen. "You're soaking wet." She pulled her by the arm and Corey stumbled inside. The house felt warm and smelled of the casserole Brin had made. Made for her.

"You're so thoughtful," Corey surprised herself in saying.

"Sorry?"

Brin closed and bolted the door and then hurriedly draped a blanket over her.

"The casserole. The dinners. Bringing me leftovers well after I'd finished the job."

Brin held the blanket ends together below Corey's chin. "I remembered what you liked."

"Yes," Corey said.

"You're shivering," Brin said.

But Corey didn't care. She was seeing in Brin's eyes what she'd seen before.

Mutual attraction.

CHAPTER TWENTY-ONE

Brin swallowed as she stared into Corey's eyes. The irises were ablaze, burning a fierce furnace-like heat into her. It didn't seem to matter that Corey was dripping wet with ice cold rain. The heat coming off her was palpable.

"You didn't have to come over here to tell me that," Brin said with a nervous laugh. "I just remembered what meals you liked is all."

Corey stood silent, dripping rain on the wood floor. Brin noticed she didn't have on a coat or her usual ball cap. It was as if she'd just run out the door, intent on doing what, she wasn't sure.

But her heart leapt at the possibilities.

"I didn't come here just to tell you that," Corey said.

"You didn't?"

"No."

Brin hesitated. "Then…what did you come for?"

Corey shivered and Brin nearly died. Waiting.

"The roof," Corey finally said. "I came to make sure those places weren't leaking."

"Oh." Brin blinked and felt the slight pulse of disappointment begin to wash through her. "They're fine. I've been checking."

"Yeah?"

"Yes. You did a great job."

"That's good."

Corey shivered again and Brin wasn't sure what to do. She wasn't sure if that was all Corey wanted to say or not. Something told her it wasn't so she followed her instincts and her instinct was to get her out of those wet clothes.

"Come on, let's get you into something warmer."

Brin tugged on her hand, but Corey stopped her. "Laken," she said. "Where is she?"

"She's asleep. She fell asleep about half an hour ago with her headphones on."

"Oh, okay."

"Why?"

"Because I want to talk to you."

Brin's stomach flipped. "You do?"

"Yes."

"Don't you want to get into some warmer clothes?"

"No."

Brin searched her eyes and suddenly she knew what she wanted to talk about.

"You don't owe me an explanation about Dawn."

"I do."

Brin held up her palm. "No, Corey, you don't."

She tried to walk away, her stomach now tightening. How could she have thought Corey had come for something else? God, she was so dense sometimes.

Corey reached out and gently gripped her arm. "Please, Brin, I do."

"Then just say it," Brin said, losing her patience. It was already killing her to consider. To even imagine her being back with Dawn. Why Corey had to come to say it directly to her face was something she didn't understand. "Say it, Corey, and then go."

Corey reared back a little as if the statement had hit her. "Okay." She stammered and seemed to be searching for the right words. "Dawn's presence today was a surprise. An *unwelcome* surprise."

Brin waited. She wasn't sure what she meant. "So, what? You're saying you didn't want her there?"

"I don't want her anywhere near me."

Brin ran a hand through her hair. "Okay."

"No, you don't understand. I don't want *her*."

"You don't?"

Corey shook her head. "No, I don't." She drew Brin closer. "And damn it, call me crazy for saying this, but I can't help it. Brin…I want you."

Brin felt her breath escape her. She forced down another swallow as she stared into her stormy eyes. "You…do?"

"Yes."

"Oh, my God."

Corey appeared lost, confused. "What does that mean?"

"It means—I don't know. I'm—Corey—"

But Corey leaned in and kissed her with the warmest, softest lips she'd ever felt. If she could melt, she most definitely would've, right then, right there, on her living room floor. She didn't melt, however, but instead fell into Corey as if she had no bones. Corey held her tight, the cold, wet rain penetrating Brin's clothes to chill her skin. But Brin didn't care; she was too caught up in the roaring fire burning between them.

"Corey," she let out. "We—shouldn't."

"Why not?"

But Brin had no answer.

Corey drew away and looked at her. "I say we give them all something to talk about."

Brin laughed a little, her nerves causing butterflies to fly wild and untamed in her belly.

"I—we—"

"Shh." Corey pressed her finger to her lips. "Do you want me to leave?"

Brin didn't hesitate. "No."

"Then what do you want?"

"Right now? I want to get you out of those wet clothes."

Corey smiled. "Here, I'll help you." She shrugged off the blanket and peeled off her sweatshirt, baring a lean, muscular chest and see-through white bra.

Brin bit her lower lip, suddenly feeling shy as she fumbled with Corey's belt buckle. Corey stilled her hands and helped her, unfastening her belt. Then she stepped out of her jeans, boots, and socks and stood there before her in her bra and underwear.

"You wear boy briefs," Brin said, nearly salivating at the gloriousness of her lithe body.

"I do," Corey said, tugging her close once again. "Now, let's see what you wear." She carefully lifted Brin's sweater up and over her body. She wore no bra so her round breasts were full and free. Brin wanted so badly for Corey to touch them, so she grabbed her wrists and brought her hands up to her.

"You don't wear anything it seems," Corey whispered as she began lightly grazing her breasts with the backs of her fingers. Brin shuddered and a hot surge of wetness shot down between her legs.

Oh, God it had been so long.

Too long.

And Corey knew just what to do, where to touch and how.

"Corey," she breathed. "Take me to my bedroom."

Corey lifted her with ease and Brin wrapped her legs around her and hugged her neck. They headed for the bedroom, safely lit by the night light in the hallway. Corey set her down and Brin quickly stood and kissed her. This time Corey lightly teased with her tongue, asking for permission. Brin granted it and groaned into her as Corey fully explored her mouth, as if capturing all that she could. Nearly overcome with raw desire, Brin quickly pushed her away and pulled her bra up over her head. Then she removed her boy briefs all while Corey watched, her eyes still ablaze.

Corey was now completely nude. She took Brin's breath away.

Brin couldn't help but stare at her. "I've never been with a woman like you."

"Like me?"

"Yes, so strong."

"It's the ranch work."

"It does wonders for your body."

"What is it that does wonders for yours?" Corey asked, drawing her closer once again. She fumbled with Brin's jeans and then slid them down her legs along with her underwear. "Because it is fantastic."

Brin laughed a little. "I sit and I write."

Corey straightened after removing her socks. "You write?"

"Mm-hm."

"And what is it that you write?"

"I—it's not important."

"But I want to know. I want to know you."

"You sure?"

"Absolutely." Corey stroked her cheek. "Now tell me."

Brin closed her eyes. "I—" She opened them. "Why don't I just show you?"

"Show me?"

"Uh-huh."

She shoved Corey back on the bed and then climbed in next to her. They settled under the covers and Corey looked at her, grinning from ear to ear.

"You write about sex?"

"Would you still want me if I said yes?"

"I would more than want you."

"Then the answer is yes."

"Then I definitely think you should show me."

"Mm, okay then." Brin traced her fingers down Corey's chest to her taut abdomen. Then she circled her center, teasing the soft curls. "Relax," she whispered while kissing her along her neck and earlobe.

Corey shuddered. "It's difficult. It's been a while."

"Here, let me help."

Brin eased her legs open by carefully grazing her fingers up and down her inner thighs. Then she returned back to her mound and teased her there as she'd done before.

Corey visibly relaxed and let out a long sigh.

"Does that feel good?"

"It's driving me mad," she said, causing Brin to laugh.

"That's the point. To get you going."

"Oh, I'm going alright."

"Mm, I can see that you are." Brin planted light kisses along her reddening chest and throat just before she slid her fingers into her wet folds. Corey moaned and came up off the bed, gripping her wrist.

"Shh," Brin said, stroking her slowly. "It's okay."

"It's better than okay," Corey rasped.

"Even better," Brin said, smiling down at her. "Now, what to do next?" She knelt and took Corey's hard nipple into her mouth. Corey cried out this time and arched her back.

"Brin," she said, tightening her hand in her hair. "Oh, God."

Brin sucked her slowly, lightly, then matched the rhythm of her hand by moving her tongue in circles around her nipple as she did the same to her clitoris, just ever so slightly grazing the edges.

"Oh, my fucking God," Corey let out and clenched her eyes.

"God, you are a sight," Brin said, loving the way her face looked as pleasure crashed over it. "So beautiful."

"I want you," Corey said.

"You've got me," Brin said, kissing her deeply.

"No," Corey said as they pulled apart. "I want you now."

"Shh, in a minute."

"But—"

Brin increased her speed and sucked hard on her nipple. Corey could no longer speak, she just kept letting out raspy cries that left Brin burning alive with want and desire. She circled her hand and sucked her nipple, and then as Corey got close to climax, she changed it up and stroked her full-on and blew on her breast, watching the nipple bunch in response.

"Fuck!" Corey said. "Oh, fuck." She grabbed her head and shook it from side to side. Her hips began to buck.

Brin smiled down at her and leaned in close to her ear, thoroughly enjoying all that she was seeing.

"Come," she whispered.

And Corey came.

She sat up and let out a long, raspy, impossibly throaty cry and pulsed there in the moment taking all that she could. Then seconds later, she thrust back onto the bed and convulsed, the pleasure now almost too much to bear. Brin recognized it all, knew exactly what to do and when. Just like how Corey knew how to touch her.

She reveled in it and drew the pleasure out of her for as long as she could.

And just as she was nuzzling her neck and kissing her face, telling her she was the most exquisite thing she'd ever seen, a little voice came from down the hallway.

"Auntie?"

CHAPTER TWENTY-TWO

Brin sat up.

Corey stilled and focused. "What was that?"

"Shh."

They heard it again, coming from down the hallway.

"Auntie?"

Brin covered her mouth. "Oh, my God, she's calling for me. Corey, she's calling for me!" She stood and hurriedly shrugged into a robe.

"That's great," Corey said, pulling the covers up tight around her. "Should I get dressed?"

"No, no. I'll be right back."

Corey eased back and waited, her flesh still pulsing between her legs. Sweat coated her chest and she wiped some from her brow. From down the hall she could hear Brin with Laken. They were doing something in the kitchen.

After a few long moments, Corey sat up and slung her legs over the bed. She found another robe and slid into it and then walked down the hallway to see what was going on. When she reached the kitchen, she found Brin and Laken at the table with a bowl of Cheerios in front of Laken. Brin was pouring the milk and when she saw Corey, she smiled.

"We're going to try some milk in our cereal," she said.

"Oh." Corey walked to the table. "Mind if I sit?"

"Please. Would you like some Cheerios?"

"No, thanks. Hey, Laken. How are you?"

Laken, who was busy carefully balancing cereal onto her spoon, nodded.

"That's good," Corey said. "I like it when you're well."

"Say, we're better than good," Brin said, grinning. "Aren't we?" She squeezed Laken's hand and then reached for Corey's. "And how are you, Corey?"

"I'd say better than good."

"I'd say so, too."

Corey kissed her hand. She sat back and took in the moment. She was with Brin and Laken, just sitting and watching Laken eat, and yet nothing had ever felt more right. She imagined sitting with them, just like this, at breakfast and at dinner every night. The thought warmed her and she couldn't help but smile.

The phone rang, however, piercing her thoughts.

Brin appeared just as startled. "Who could that be?" She rose and retrieved her phone from the counter.

"Oh, no," she said.

"Don't tell me." Corey felt her whole body stiffen.

"It's Miley."

"Jesus."

"What should I do?"

"Don't answer it."

"If I don't answer she might just show up."

"And that would be bad considering I'm here, right? And in one of your bath robes?"

"Well, it wouldn't be good."

Brin answered the phone.

"Miley, hi…No, no we're fine." She looked to Corey. "The roof held. Yes. All is well."

Corey heated at the mere suggestion that her work wouldn't stand up against the storm.

"No. No, that's not necessary. I'm sure everything is fine up there…Okay, Miley, I'm going to let you go now. I have to tend to Laken. Okay, good-bye."

She ended the call and let out a long breath.

"I think that will stop her from coming over."

"Right." Corey was still heated, but now it was about more than Miley. It was the possibility that she was going to have to be Brin's secret. She was too old to be someone's secret. She couldn't go back in the closet. Not after she'd fought so hard to come out all those years ago.

She stood. Brin looked alarmed.

"Where are you going?"

"Home."

"But why?" She crossed to her and tugged on the arm of the robe. "Don't you want to stay?" She'd lowered her voice and narrowed her eyes in a seductive manner. It stirred Corey but it did little to douse her concerns.

Corey drew away, not wanting to talk in front of Laken. "I'll call you tomorrow, okay?"

"But—"

"Everything is fine. Just tend to Laken."

She left her in the kitchen and hurried to the bedroom to get her bra and underwear. Then she yanked on her wet clothes and gathered her keys in the living room. She shivered as the cold from the damp clothes permeated her skin.

"You're not even dry," Brin said from the entryway to the living room.

"I'm fine. Just a little chilly."

"Are you really leaving?"

Corey turned from the door and gave her a wistful smile. "I am."

"Okay," Brin said. "Good night."

"Night."

Corey walked out into sporadic rain. It fell upon her as if lightly punishing her with pinpricks for leaving so shortly after lovemaking. She knew it was wrong, rude even, but she just couldn't stay. She needed to talk to Brin and she couldn't do that in front of Laken.

No, now was not the time.

She crawled in her truck and cursed herself the whole way home.

What had she been thinking? She'd known Brin wanted privacy. That she didn't want to be outed. So, what had she thought would come of them making love?

I saw the look in her eyes, saw that she wanted me too, and I couldn't resist. I just couldn't help myself.

She banged the heel of her hand on the steering wheel. "Damn it."

She'd lost the careful control she'd had over her life. The "no dating after Dawn" rule apparently thrown out the window.

How could I?

After all the pain I've been through?

Fuck.

She hit her hand again.

And now Brin was involved, and she'd looked at her with such sadness and confusion when she'd left.

So, what was she to do now?

Had she just ruined everything between her and Brin? Could they even remain friends?

She didn't know.

She didn't know anything.

Not anymore.

❖

"You gonna answer that or not?" Grey asked as they raked up the remaining dead pumpkins and vegetation from the pumpkin patch.

"Not," Corey said, eyeing the caller ID and re-pocketing her phone.

"Who in the hell are you ignoring then? That phone's been ringing since sunup yesterday."

"No one."

"No one?"

"It's nothing." Corey dumped another rake full in the wheelbarrow and then wheeled it over to dump in the trailer to be taken to compost. It was hard, time-consuming work, but she was enjoying it. Mainly because it was keeping her mind off Brin.

She wheeled the barrow back to where she and Grey were working and caught Grey staring at her.

"What?" Corey asked.

"You know what."

"No, I really don't." She grabbed her rake and started in again, her breath coming out in white clouds. The day was gray and overcast, a noticeable chill in the air. But as it was she was sweating and that's how she preferred it.

"You went and did it, didn't you?"

"Did what?"

Grey didn't move and Corey looked up at her. She nodded back toward Brin's.

"You slept with her."

Corey returned to raking without giving her the satisfaction of an answer.

Grey didn't seem to need it.

"Yup. I thought as much."

Corey raked harder. "How do you know I'm not just ignoring Dawn?"

Grey laughed. "Because she wouldn't waste her time calling you. She'd just show up. That woman has no social graces."

Corey kept raking. Damn it. Grey was right. But she wasn't about to let her know that.

"And there's another reason why I know it's Brin you're ignoring."

"Yeah, why's that?"

"Because she's headed this way right now. And she don't look none too happy."

Corey straightened and looked back toward Brin's. Grey was right. She was almost to the patch.

"Shit," Corey mumbled.

She dropped her rake and hurried to her, wanting to talk to her out of Grey's earshot.

"Hey," Corey said, upon walking up to her.

"Hey?"

"Hi?"

"You're real funny." She crossed her arms over her chest and the look of hurt on her face made Corey's insides twist.

"I'm sorry," Corey said.

"For what? For not calling me like you said you would? Or for ignoring my calls? Or for standing there like I'm some annoying stranger? Which one is it?"

"I'm not ignoring you. I've just been—"

"Save the bullshit for someone else, Corey, because I'm not buying it."

"Brin, I'm really sorry. I am. I just—we need to talk."

She scoffed. "Don't bother. I know what this is. It's a brush-off. We fucked and you're brushing me off."

"No, that's not it." Corey took a step toward her, wanting so badly to hold her in her arms.

"Then what is it?"

"It's—I can't be your secret."

Brin blinked at her. "What?"

"I can't be your secret, Brin."

"I—see." She threw up her hands. "So that's it, then? You're just going to write me off?"

"You don't want to be out."

"No, I don't, but it has nothing to do with you. And if you would've bothered answering your damn phone and actually talking to me, you'd know that. You'd know my story and know why. But you chose not to. You chose to fucking ignore me like a one-night stand you'd rather forget about."

"Brin—"

"No, Corey. No." She dropped her hands in defeat. "Just, no." She turned and walked away and Corey hurried after her.

"Brin, wait. Brin!"

But Brin held up her palm, letting her know she didn't want to be followed.

Corey stopped her pursuit and watched her go. She watched her raise her hand to her face as if she were wiping away tears and Corey's heart bled for her. She yearned to go after her, but she held back, giving her her space.

Brin didn't want to be followed, just like she didn't want to be outed.

Corey removed her hat and slapped it against her thigh. She walked back to the patch and to Grey and picked up her rake.

"Don't even say it," Corey said, in no mood to hear Grey tell her she should've known better.

"I think that little lady just said it all."

"You heard?"

"Hard not to."

"Shit. There really is no privacy in this damn town."

"You really sleep with her and then disappear on her?"

Corey leaned on her rake, her guts feeling like they were gonna spill out all over the earth.

"Yeah. Yeah, I did."

Grey tsked. "Never pegged you for one to do that."

"Well, you don't know the circumstances. Brin—she doesn't want to be outed and I can't be her secret."

"Says who? You? Since when are you against privacy? And as far as I heard, you didn't even give her a chance to explain."

"There's nothing to say."

"I know what this is," Grey said.

"What?"

"You're chicken shit. And you're using this as an excuse to keep from getting close to her."

"The only shit around here is coming from you because you're full of it."

"Uh-huh. I think you really like this woman and that scares you. Scares you to death. Especially after seeing Dawn the other night."

Corey threw down her rake and walked away.

"Where you going?" Grey called out.

"Somewhere far away from you." Corey heard Grey say something else but she couldn't make it out and she didn't stick around to find out what it was. Instead, she headed for the stables where she found Lily in her stall.

"Hey, girl," she said softly as she nuzzled her nose. "How ya doing?"

Lily bumped her, as if answering.

"Yeah, I know. Life can be a doozy, can't it?"

She stroked her flank and thought of little Laken and how much she'd probably love Lily. The thought caused her to laugh a little. Here she was arguing with Brin, trying half-heartedly to end things, and she was still thinking of her and Laken.

Brin and Laken.

Laken and Brin.

Would she ever be able to stop?

CHAPTER TWENTY-THREE

Brin thanked the delivery man and set the heavy box on the coffee table to cut the tape with a pair of scissors. She and Laken had been making paper turkeys by tracing Laken's hand onto some construction paper, and now Laken was sitting lotus-style on the shag rug coloring them with bits of scraps strewn about.

The day was cold but sunny, serene and quiet, much to Brin's dismay. She'd preferred a more hectic day, one that would keep her super busy and focused on the task at hand, rather than a day like today when all she could think about was Corey. And every time she did, her chest tightened and her heart felt like it was being squeezed by a vise. She just didn't understand Corey's sudden coldness. She'd given her a good reason for retreating, but to not even talk to her? It just didn't sound like Corey.

I guess I didn't really know her after all.

And that's why I should've kept my nose to the grindstone and focused solely on Laken and work.

Work. It had been going well. She'd managed to complete her latest manuscript right on time, despite the chaos of losing Breana. And now here it was, staring back at her from the box. Her latest book. A historical romance. A *lesbian* historical romance.

Shit.

She'd told Corey that she was a writer. That she wrote about sex. Would she say anything? She didn't think Corey to be the type, since she seemed to hate rumors too. But then again she'd never thought Corey the type to turn so cold so quickly either.

God, I hope she doesn't say anything.

I can't go through what I went through before.

She retrieved a book from the box and sat back to examine it. Laken joined her on the couch with a paper turkey in her hand. She gave it to her.

"Thank you, love. It's wonderful. A wonderful turkey."

"Turkey," Laken said.

"Yes." Brin kissed the top of her head and Laken eyed the book. "You want to see? This is Auntie's book."

She let Laken have it and they snuggled back into the couch as Brin read the cover to her and then the dedication.

To my sister, Breana.

This one's for you.

"I can't read a whole lot more to you, love. This book is for grown-ups."

Laken looked up at her.

"My book?"

"Yes, why don't you go get one of your books from your bedroom and we'll read it in here?"

Laken crawled from the couch and headed off toward her bedroom. Brin traced her finger across the cover of the romance, recalling how her publisher had raved over the book and told her of the stellar advance reviews. Her stomach knotted at the possibility of the book doing really well. While as a writer she wanted very much for her work to be liked and admired, she also valued her privacy. And the thought of having to do interviews or go to readings, worried her. If she did those things, she wouldn't be able to hide for very long. All she could do was pray that no one in Utopia read lesbian romances.

Laken ran back into the room and plopped on the couch with her favorite book and her stuffed whale. But just then the doorbell rang. Brin rose to answer it.

She sighed as she looked out the peephole. She'd hoped, for a split second, that it might be Corey coming by to talk.

Wishful thinking.

No, instead of Corey standing there it was Miley Roberts. And she appeared to have another casserole in her hands.

Brin unbolted the door and opened it.

"Howdy, neighbor," Miley said with a big grin. "I brought you a lovely chicken casserole. Thought you might want to eat this for the next couple of days since you'll probably be cooking up a storm on Thanksgiving."

Brin immediately knew it was a ploy to find out what she was doing for Thanksgiving. She didn't take the bait. Instead, she just took the casserole.

"Oh, well, thank you. You're so thoughtful, Miley, really."

Miley stood there smiling. Waiting.

Brin inwardly cursed.

"Would you like to come in?"

"Why thank you, I think I would. It's mighty cold out," she said as she shrugged her way inside, already tugging at her scarf.

"Well, hi, little Laken. How are you?" She called her by the correct name for once, but Laken looked up with complete disinterest.

That's my girl.

Brin almost laughed.

"My, how she's grown in just a short amount of time."

"She should be. She's eating much better."

"Yes, I've heard that she's improving a lot."

Brin cringed. She didn't like Miley discussing Laken's ability to do anything. Miley always made it sound like Laken was less than. And that pissed Brin off to no end.

"Laken, why don't you take your book and go in your room and read for a little while?"

She figured the less she had to be around Miley Roberts, the better.

Laken took her book and slid off the couch.

"In fact, why don't you put on your headphones and listen to your music?"

Laken ran down the hallway in her excited manner.

"She's adorable," Miley said.

Brin wanted to cringe again. Nothing Miley ever said felt genuine. She wondered what she wanted.

"Well, as you can see, my roof held up."

Miley blinked at her, then looked up, as if the leak had been in the living room.

"Yes, I see."

Brin rolled her eyes. Miley didn't, however, see that.

"What can I do for you, Miley?"

"Well, funny you should ask."

Oh, God.

"Jimmy and I wanted to extend an invitation to you and little Laken for Thanksgiving dinner this Thursday. We'll have all the trimmings and we know you don't have any family here to speak of."

"I have—friends," Brin countered.

Miley smiled. "Word around town is that you and Corey are no longer…friends. So, Jimmy and I thought we'd extend an invitation. After all, it's the right thing to do."

Yes, and you're all about doing right, aren't you? Jesus, how does she know? I only fought with Corey a few days ago.

"Well, thank you, Miley, but Laken and I have other plans already."

"Oh?"

"Yes."

She stood firm, not about to share those plans. Not because she wanted them kept private or anything. But because she didn't want to give Miley Roberts the satisfaction in knowing.

After a long silence, Miley cleared her throat. "Well, I hope it's nice, wherever it is."

Brin smiled. "Thank you. I hope you have a nice Thanksgiving as well. Oh, and I have two of your casserole dishes in the kitchen. I'll be right back."

Brin hurried off to the kitchen and retrieved the dishes from the cabinet. Then she returned to the living room to find Miley reading the back cover of her latest release.

Brin nearly dropped the dishes and Miley jerked and put down the book as she reappeared.

Brin shoved the dishes in her hands. "Here ya go," she said, backing her to the door and opening it. "Thanks again for stopping by and for the casserole. I'm sure we'll enjoy it."

"Oh—well, okay," Miley stammered as she backed out the door.

"Talk soon," Brin said and closed the door in her face. She bolted it shut and then ran to grab the book off the couch. She scanned the back quickly and her heart sank. Though she wrote using a pen name, a photo of her was used on the back cover. It wasn't a close-up and she was wearing sunglasses, but someone who knew her could still tell it was her.

"Fuck!"

She threw the book down and paced. Memories of her past flooded her and she felt sick. She couldn't go through that again. And she wasn't about to let Laken go through it.

She wished like hell she'd opted not to do the author photo. But her publisher had insisted that readers like to know their authors, and since she was private in every other area of her writing world, a distant photo donning sunglasses seemed like a good compromise.

"Fuck!"

She sat and grabbed her head. How could she've been so stupid? Leaving the box out with Miley Roberts there? Jesus.

There was no doubt now. It would be all over town.

Just like before.

And just like before, she'd want to flee.

With the way things were going with Corey, the idea of fleeing again didn't sound so bad.

CHAPTER TWENTY-FOUR

Corey paced back and forth in front of the fireplace. She couldn't sit down and she couldn't rest. Not until she figured out what to say to Brin.

Inside her chest, her heart hammered, and her mouth was so dry she could hardly swallow.

That's what it feels like when you feel responsible.

But I'm not responsible!

Tell Brin that.

"Damn it!" She stopped and stood in front of the fire, leaning on the mantel. She stared at the dancing flames wishing she could get lost in them and fall asleep. But as it was, she hadn't slept for two days. Not since she'd been to town and heard all about Brin's occupation as a lesbian romance author. An *erotic* lesbian romance author.

It seemed the news was everywhere and people all over town were buying up her latest release online to see what all the fuss was about. Word also had it that Brin wouldn't even venture into town. The last person who'd seen her was Flick. He'd said she'd come in for some nails for her baseboards and that she hardly spoke and looked flat-out exhausted and awful. Said she wouldn't say what she was doing for Thanksgiving.

Corey pushed away from the fireplace. She didn't know how, but someone said that Miley had started the rumor. How could Miley have known? It didn't make sense. Surely Brin wouldn't have told her. No, Miley found out on her own, guaranteed. But Corey worried that Brin would think it was her who started the rumors, because she'd told her she was a writer. And she couldn't let Brin think that. She just couldn't.

"You about ready?" Ryan asked as he walked into the room from the garage.

They were due at Grey's soon for Thanksgiving dinner.

"I don't want to go," she said, staring back into the fire.

"Oh. You thinking about Brin again?"

She didn't bother arguing. "Yeah, I'm thinking about Brin again."

"Why don't you just go talk to her?"

Corey laughed. "Because she'd slam the door in my face, that's why."

"I seriously doubt that," Ryan said, removing his cowboy hat. He looked and smelled nice in his black Stetson hat and matching button-down shirt. She wondered if he was going to see his girlfriend later after dinner.

"It can't hurt to try," he said. "And I know she cares about you."

"How do you know that?"

He shrugged. "Because she stopped smiling."

Corey looked at him and he explained.

"In town, I saw her shortly after you two…ended things and she wasn't smiling. I even said hello and she just hung her head. Now I know I'm not old enough to know a whole lot, but, Corey, damn it, that woman looked heart broke."

Corey stabbed at some logs with the poker.

"She thinks I told everyone about her writing."

"Why do you think that?"

"Because I'm the only one she told about it and now it's all over town."

"That was Miley Roberts's doing."

Corey turned. "Yes, but how did Miley find out?"

He shrugged again. "I don't know. But I know you didn't tell her. You wouldn't do that."

"No, I wouldn't."

"Brin knows that, too."

Corey shook her head. "I don't think she does."

A door opened and closed behind Ryan and Whip barked as they all searched for the source. Corey nearly dropped the poker as she saw Dawn strut in.

"Happy Thanksgiving," she said with a smile. "Hey, Ryan. Haven't seen you in a long while. In fact, last time I saw you you was this high." She held her hand out to about chest level.

"Yeah, and last time I saw you, you were just high." He turned and looked to Corey. "Should I wait in the truck?"

"No. This won't take long." Corey didn't want to be left alone with her. She had no idea why she was there.

"What do you want, Dawn? And since when do you just walk in my house?"

"Oh, well I just thought you might want me to."

"Why would I want you to?"

She smirked and walked closer, bypassing Ryan and Whip. "Because I heard about you and that little girlfriend of yours. Heard you broke up. And with the way you trembled in my arms last time, I knew you still loved me. If Grey hadn't butted in we'd already be back together, now wouldn't we?"

Corey looked her dead in the eye. "No. We wouldn't."

"Oh, come on, Corey. Don't tell me you don't love me."

Corey swallowed. "I. Don't."

"She doesn't," Ryan said.

"You stay out of this, little boy," Dawn said, whipping around to look at Ryan.

"Don't speak to him that way," Corey said. "That little boy is a man and he's a much better person than you are or ever will be."

Dawn looked as though she'd been struck. But she seemed to have recovered quickly.

"You don't know me, Corey Durand," she said. "I've changed."

Corey let out a laugh. "No, you haven't."

"How do you know? You won't spend any time with me."

"Because you just keep showing up uninvited, thinking that somehow I'll be glad to see you. No, Dawn, you're as narcissistic as you ever were."

She didn't seem to have a response and Corey's phone rang.

Corey fished out her phone and looked at the caller ID. She answered right away.

"Corey?" It was Brin and she sounded upset.

"Yes? What is it? What's wrong?" Her heart leapt to her throat.

"It's Laken. I can't find her. Please tell me she's with you."

Corey hurried to the back door and pulled it open. She stepped out onto the vast patio and scanned the grounds. And that's when she saw her. Little Laken. Chasing after Wiley the goat who must've escaped his pen. They were headed for the silo.

"She's here," Corey said. "She's headed for the silo. I'm going after her."

"I'll be right there," Brin said.

Corey pocketed her phone and called back to Ryan. "I'm going after Laken and I may need your help."

Both Ryan and Dawn stepped outside to look.

Ryan nodded at her and Corey took off at a dead sprint. She heard Ryan running behind her. Whip bypassed her quickly, somehow understanding what they were after.

Please don't see the ladder. Please don't see the ladder.

But Laken did. As soon as she came upon the silo, she stopped and looked up, Wiley seemingly long forgotten. She immediately stretched, trying to grab onto the lower ladder rung.

Don't do it.

Don't do it.

She reached it and pulled herself up and began climbing the ladder to the silo.

Damn it!

Whip reached the silo seconds later and began barking up at her.

Corey ran harder, her boots slipping and sliding in some areas from the mud. When she reached the silo she was astonished to see just how high Laken had managed to climb.

Corey didn't even stop to catch her breath or to check for Ryan. She just called back to him.

"Call 911! I'm going up." She started climbing, her boots slipping on the rungs.

"Hold on, Laken, I'm coming."

Laken, who was nearing the top, stopped and looked down at her. She began to cry.

"It's okay," she said, trying to soothe her. But Laken was now clinging to the ladder, hugging it with both arms. She was truly terrified now that she'd looked down.

At least she's not climbing anymore.

Corey continued to climb, but she slowed her pace. Laken was frightened so she moved slowly and spoke softly to her.

"It's okay, sweetie. It's me, Corey, and I'm coming to get you so we can get down from here, okay?"

Laken cried harder and turned her head, refusing to look at her.

Down below, Corey heard a vehicle and voices. She looked down and saw that Brin had arrived and she was standing beside Ryan and Dawn, her mouth covered with her hands.

"Corey, help her!" she shouted.

"I am!"

"Climb faster! Oh, my God!" She began to cry and Corey gripped the ladder harder and moved a little faster while Laken wasn't looking.

She spoke softly to her again as she came up below her. Laken looked down at her and sobbed. Her body trembled.

"Laken, it's okay," Corey soothed her. "Just look at me, okay? I'm right here. See? Can you feel me climbing up behind you?" She climbed up behind her and encased her with her arms on the ladder. She didn't dare look down, but she could hear more commotion on the ground. In the distance, she heard sirens. They were growing closer. Whip began to howl.

"Corey," Laken said between gulps of air.

"Yes, sweetie. I'm right here."

"Scary," she said.

"I know. But don't look down. Just do as I say. Can you do that?"

Corey didn't wait for an answer. "Okay, Laken, I need you to take a step down. Can you do that for me?"

Laken held fast to the ladder, shaking from fear and from crying.

"Stay," she said.

"Okay, we can stay right here for a few minutes. Just relax. Breathe deeply like I am."

She breathed deeply, pushing the air out loudly for Laken to follow.

"Good job."

The sirens grew closer and Corey turned to look. A firetruck and an ambulance had arrived, and Ryan was helping to direct them in. They parked close to the silo and the volunteers jumped out. One of the men was Flick. She waved them off.

"Okay, Laken. Take one more big breath and then we're going to take a step down, okay?"

They both took another breath and though Laken was still shaking, she took a tentative step down.

"Good!" Corey said. "Now, can you do it again?"

Corey moved down and Laken did the same.

"Great job, Laken. Now keep doing that, okay? I've got you. I'm right here and we're doing this together."

They slowly descended the silo, and by the time they neared the bottom, Corey's arms and legs were shaking as badly as Laken's.

When she reached the last rung, her boot slipped and she nearly fell. But she caught herself and managed to reach the ground and take Laken in her arms.

"Oh, thank God," Brin said, embracing them both in a strong hug. "Are you okay?" She asked as she took Laken from her. "Are you hurt?"

Flick came up and tried to examine her, but Laken buried her face in Brin's shoulder.

"She's okay," Corey said. "Just a little overwhelmed and frightened."

Flick nodded. "You're a very lucky young lady," he said to Laken.

Laken shook her head and pointed. "Corey," she said.

"Yes, Corey saved you, didn't she?" He laughed and backed away to tell his men that all was well.

"Hug," Laken said as she looked at Corey.

Brin laughed. "You want to hug Corey? Okay, let's hug her." They enveloped in a hug.

"Thank you," Brin whispered. "I'll never be able to repay you."

"You just did," Corey said. "With this hug."

"I'd like to do more than that," she said.

Corey drew away. "What did you have in mind?"

"This." She leaned in and kissed her. Corey blinked, totally surprised. And apparently, she wasn't the only one. Dawn balked while Laken clapped and a couple of the firemen whistled.

"I don't care who sees," Brin said. "Or who knows. I want you in our lives, Corey Durand."

"You're sure?"

"I've always wanted you. I was just too terrified to declare it for all the world to know. But now I don't care. I want the whole world to know. And I knew that the second I saw you climbing up that ladder to save Laken."

"Well, you're too late," Dawn said.

She was standing in her trademark position, hands on hips, scowl on her face. "I mean, we were going to talk, right, Corey?"

Corey pulled Brin tighter to her. "No, Dawn. There's nothing to be said. So, you need to leave. Now. And if I have to, I'll file a restraining order."

Dawn's eyes widened. "Fine. Whatever. You're boring anyway. You don't know how to have any fun."

"Not if your idea of fun is shooting up heroin, no."

Ryan chuckled and a few of the volunteer firemen did as well.

"Fine," Dawn said. "I'll go."

"Bye," Corey said.

"Bye," Laken said with a wave.

Brin laughed and kissed Laken's cheek.

Grey pulled up in her truck and jumped out, obviously having heard from Ryan about what had happened. She looked relieved to see Corey and Laken on the ground.

"Everything okay?" she asked.

"Yes," Brin said. "Everything is fine." She kissed Corey again and Grey stared as if she couldn't believe what she'd just witnessed.

Ryan just chuckled again and kicked his feet.

"Well, I guess that means we're all ready for some turkey then, doesn't it?" Grey said with a smile.

Corey winked at her and mouthed a thank you.

Brin looked at Corey with soulful eyes. "Is it really okay if we come with?"

"Absolutely."

"Good, because I really didn't want to drive down to Phoenix anyway. I would rather be here, with you. With my new family."

Corey smiled at her. "And nothing would make me happier."

CHAPTER TWENTY-FIVE

"Morning."

Brin moaned as Corey's warm mouth kissed lightly at her ear. "Mm, morning."

"How did you sleep?" Corey asked as she wrapped her arms around her.

"Did we sleep?"

Corey laughed. "Some. I think."

"Because I seem to remember a certain insatiable lover invading my bed last night."

"Really? Insatiable?"

"Oh, yes. Three times was not near enough for her. She had to have me all night long."

"Well, maybe she was making up for lost time."

"I think maybe she was."

"And that was okay with you?"

Brin laughed. "Oh, yes. More than okay. Question is, can she keep it up?"

Corey tickled her ribs and Brin howled with laughter. "Corey, stop!"

"Shh, you'll wake Laken and I want another round with you before she wakes."

"Then stop tickling me!"

Corey held up her hand and nuzzled her ear again. "Okay. Okay." She snuggled closer and spoke softly in her ear. "I'm so glad you're okay with us being together."

"I am too."

"What...you know, happened to you to make you fear being outed?"

Brin held her arms, feeling the safest she'd ever felt. She closed her eyes, remembering.

"Well, you know what I write."

"Yes."

"I was young when I first started. Young, out, and proud. And I was very proud of my work."

"As you should be."

"That's what I thought. But apparently, not everyone agreed." She opened her eyes and stroked Corey's arm. "I had this job. A really good job. I was a journalist at a local newspaper in a suburb of Phoenix. A small paper, family owned, but still I was a writer and I felt I was making a difference, one small story at a time. I was quite happy."

"But one day while having lunch with a colleague, I let it slip that I was a published novelist. You see he had been bragging about having a short story published and he was being rather obnoxious about it and a little snotty, so I told him. I didn't tell him my pen name, but I told him I wrote romance. Well, he knew I was gay, everyone did, because out and proud, right?"

"Right."

"I guess he took it upon himself to search me out. Probably wasn't difficult for him to find me. He just had to search for lesbian romance authors who live in Arizona, and bam, there I am, photo and all."

"Oh, no."

"Yeah, oh no is right. This guy proceeds to tell everyone at the paper, including my editor, who contacts the owners of the paper, who, let's just say, have a real issue with the erotic content."

"Oh, Brin."

"Uh-huh."

"Did they fire you?"

"Oh, no. Because they feared a lawsuit. So instead they made my life a living hell. I was ostracized at work. No one would talk to me and if they did, I could tell that they had already made up their minds about me based on what this guy said. He started bad-mouthing my work, said I didn't do things right, etc. I was given tasks to complete and when I did, I was told they weren't completed as instructed, even though I'd followed directions. It was just one little thing after another. My computer was confiscated, to check for illegal material. I mean you name it and they either did it to me, or tried to do it to me."

"But none of them ever confronted you about your books?"

"No."

"How did you know they'd found out?"

"Because one of my books was left on the hood of my car at work. So I knew then that he'd found me. And that was his little warning. But when I didn't quit or back down, he started with all the rest, including trying to ruin my writing career by leaving me bad reviews and spreading harmful gossip on social media. And everyone else just jumped on the bandwagon and followed his lead."

"What did you do?"

"I put up with it for weeks, trying to pull through. I applied for other jobs, but this place wouldn't give me a good reference. They would subtly bad-mouth me. I started having panic attacks before going into work. Some days I couldn't even get out of my car."

"Jesus."

"Yeah. I know. It was bad. Thankfully, my publisher understood and she encouraged me to wait out the storm. But my sales were impacted. And now that I have Laken to support you can see why I was so scared."

"I can, yes. So what happened with the job?"

"Well one day, I just decided I couldn't do it anymore. I couldn't go back. And I never did."

"Ever?"

"No. I stayed in bed for two weeks, completely traumatized and depressed. But then my sister, God bless her, came over and shoved open my curtains and yanked me out of bed and said, 'Enough of this shit. You've got to move on.' And she pushed me in the shower, turned on the cold water, and shocked me back to life."

"Wow."

"Wow is right. Breana didn't fuck around. She was all about kicking ass and continuing on, no matter the problem. That was something I kept in mind and it helped me eventually become less afraid in this case as well."

"Your sister helping you move on?"

"Yes, and to be fearless. When she first helped me, I started writing more, and even started editing on the side and I was able to make a living, not to mention sharpen my craft. I moved in with Breana when she got sick and helped her fight for as long as we could."

"And then you moved here."

"Yes."

"But you were still afraid."

"Yes, but eventually I came around. Laken brought Breana's picture up to me one night and it just clicked. I realized I needed to face this, head on and be proud of who I was and what I write, no matter the consequence."

"Even though you were afraid, you still told me."

Brin hugged her closer. “Because I was into you.”

“Oh, not because you trusted me?”

“Well, that too. But mainly because I was into you.”

Corey laughed and tickled her again briefly.

“It was a very risky thing to do, but I couldn’t stop myself. There was just something about you.”

“That’s how I felt the night I came over during the storm. I just couldn’t help myself, I had to have you.”

Brin rolled over and stared up into her eyes. “You did?”

“Yes.”

“What about now, you still want me now that you’ve had me?”

Corey smiled. “Oh, God yes.”

Brin laughed and stroked her cheek.

“As long as you’re still okay with my having you,” Corey said.

“Oh, I am.”

“Even though you’re now a hotshot author with a best-selling book?”

“Yes. Who knew this whole thing would backfire on Miley?”

“Well, it is a good book,” Corey said. “Your sales are proving that.”

“Why thank you, Ms. Durand.”

“It hasn’t gone to your head has it?”

“No.”

Corey laughed and Brin’s phone rang on the nightstand. Brin grabbed it and sighed when she saw who was calling.

“Who is it?” Corey asked.

“It’s the gossip queen.”

“Oh, no, don’t answer it.”

“Shh, give me a sec.”

She answered the call and put it on speaker. "Miley, hi."

"Well, good morning, Brin, it's a beautiful day out, isn't it?"

"Seems to be. I wouldn't know though, I'm still in bed."

"Oh, well, I hope I didn't wake you."

"You didn't."

"Good."

"So, what can I do for you?"

"Well, I was just calling to congratulate you on your book! I hear it's doing fabulously!"

"Why, thank you, Miley." Brin rolled her eyes at Corey who clenched her jaw and reddened. Brin stroked her face and smiled.

"Anywho, I was wondering if you'd do me the honor of being the guest of honor at my next party? Maybe we could even set up some sort of signing for you here at the house? I'm just so excited for you!"

Brin looked at Corey. She traced her fingers down to her lips.

"So, you're calling me because my book is doing so well? Is that it?"

"Well, yes and I'd like to throw you a party to celebrate. How does that sound?"

"The answer is no, Miley. Thank you, but no."

"No? Well, I'm sorry to hear that. Is there anything little ol' me can do to change your mind?"

"Yes. There is. You can let me go now."

"Let you go now?"

"Yes. You see I need to go now so I can give you and all the rest of this town something to talk about."

"Something to talk about?"

"I'm going to hang up the phone and make love to Corey Durand. Right here, right now."

Miley gasped.

"Bye, Miley. Talk soon!" She ended the call and tossed the phone aside.

"That was a very brave thing to do, my love," Corey said, leaning toward her. "Did you mean it?"

"You know I did."

"Then show me."

"I'd be happy to."

THE END

About the Author

An avid reader from early childhood, Ronica Black spends a great deal of time with her nose in a book, whether that be one she's working on herself or another author's. When she's not reading or writing, she's spending time with her little rescue dog, Frankie, hiking, or exploring the great state of Arizona with friends. She also enjoys painting, drawing, and doing anything creative. She lives in the greater Phoenix area.

Books Available from Bold Strokes Books

A Long Way to Fall by Elle Spencer. A ski lodge, two strong-willed women, and a family feud that brings them together, but will it also tear them apart? (978-1-63679-005-3)

Barnabas Bopwright Saves the City by J. Marshall Freeman. When he uncovers a terror plot to destroy the city he loves, 15-year-old Barnabas Bopwright realizes it's up to him to save his home and bring deadly secrets into the light before it's too late. (978-1-63679-152-4)

Forever by Kris Bryant. When Savannah Edwards is invited to be the next bachelorette on the dating show When Sparks Fly, she'll show the world that finding true love on television can happen. (978-1-63679-029-9)

Ice on Wheels by Aurora Rey. All's fair in love and roller derby. That's Riley Fauchet's motto, until a new job lands her at the same company—and on the same team—as her rival Brooke Landry, the frosty jammer for the Big Easy Bruisers. (978-1-63679-179-1)

Inherit the Lightning by Bud Gundy. Darcy O'Brien and his sisters learn they are about to inherit an immense fortune, but a family mystery about to unravel after seventy years threatens to destroy everything. (978-1-63679-199-9)

Perfect Rivalry by Radclyffe. Two women set out to win the same career-making goal, but it's love that may turn out to be the final prize. (978-1-63679-216-3)

Something to Talk About by Ronica Black. Can quiet ranch owner Corey Durand give up her peaceful life and allow her feisty new neighbor into her heart? Or will past loss, present suitors, and town gossip ruin a long-awaited chance at love? (978-1-63679-114-2)

With a Minor in Murder by Karis Walsh. In the world of academia, police officer Clare Sawyer and professor Libby Hart team up to solve a murder. (978-1-63679-186-9)

Writer's Block by Ali Vali. Wyatt and Hayley might be made for each other if only they can get through noisy neighbors, the historic society, at-odds future plans, and all the secrets hidden in Wyatt's walls. (978-1-63679-021-3)

Cold Blood by Genevieve McCluer. Maybe together, Kalila and Dorenia have a chance of taking down the vampires who have eluded them all these years. And maybe, in each other, they can find a love worth living for. (978-1-63679-195-1)

Greener Pastures by Aurora Rey. When city girl and CPA Audrey Adams finds herself tending her aunt's farm, will Rowan Marshall—the charming cider maker next door—turn out to be her saving grace or the bane of her existence? (978-1-63679-116-6)

Grounded by Amanda Radley. For a second chance, Olivia and Emily will need to accept their mistakes, learn to communicate properly, and with a little help from five-year-old Henry, fall madly in love all over again. Sequel to Flight SQA016. (978-1-63679-241-5)

Journey's End by Amanda Radley. In this heartwarming conclusion to the Flight series, Olivia and Emily must finally decide what they want, what they need, and how to follow the dreams of their hearts. (978-1-63679-233-0)

Pursued: Lillian's Story by Felice Picano. Fleeing a disastrous marriage to the Lord Exchequer of England, Lillian of Ravenglass reveals an incident-filled, often bizarre, tale of great wealth and power, perfidy, and betrayal. (978-1-63679-197-5)

Secret Agent by Michelle Larkin. CIA agent Peyton North embarks on a global chase to apprehend rogue agent Zoey Blackwood, but her commitment to the mission is tested as the sparks between them ignite and their sizzling attraction approaches a point of no return. (978-1-63555-753-4)

Something Between Us by Krystina Rivers. A decade after her heart was broken under Don't Ask, Don't Tell, Kirby runs into her first love and has to decide if what's still between them is enough to heal her broken heart. (978-1-63679-135-7)

Sugar Girl by Emma L McGeown. Having traded in traditional romance for the perks of Sugar Dating, Ciara Reilly not only enjoys the no-strings-attached arrangement, she's also a hit with her clients. That is until she meets the beautiful entrepreneur Charlie Keller who makes her want to go sugar-free. (978-1-63679-156-2)

The Business of Pleasure by Ronica Black. Editor in chief Valerie Raffield is quickly becoming smitten by Lennox, the graphic artist she's hired to work remotely. But when Lennox doesn't show for their first face-to-face meeting, Valerie's heart and her business may be in jeopardy. (978-1-63679-134-0)

The Hummingbird Sanctuary by Erin Zak. The Hummingbird Sanctuary, Colorado's hottest resort destination: Come for the mountains, stay for the charm, and enjoy the drama as Olive, Eleanor, and Harriet figure out the meaning of true friendship. (978-1-63679-163-0)

The Witch Queen's Mate by Jennifer Karter. Barra and Silvi must overcome their ingrained hatred and prejudice to use Barra's magic and save both their peoples, not just from slavery, but destruction. (978-1-63679-202-6)

With a Twist by Georgia Beers. Starting over isn't easy for Amelia Martini. When the irritatingly cheerful Kirby Dupress comes into her life will Amelia be brave enough to go after the love she really wants? (978-1-63555-987-3)

Business of the Heart by Claire Forsythe. When a hopeless romantic meets a tough-as-nails cynic, they'll need to overcome the wounds of the past to discover that their hearts are the most important business of all. (978-1-63679-167-8)

Dying for You by Jenny Frame. Can Victorija Dred keep an age-old vow and fight the need to take blood from Daisy Macdougall? (978-1-63679-073-2)

Exclusive by Melissa Brayden. Skylar Ruiz lands the TV reporting job of a lifetime, but is she willing to sacrifice it all for the love of her longtime crush, anchorwoman Carolyn McNamara? (978-1-63679-112-8)

Her Duchess to Desire by Jane Walsh. An up-and-coming interior designer seeks to create a happily ever after with an intriguing duchess, proving that love never goes out of fashion. (978-1-63679-065-7)

Murder on Monte Vista by David S. Pederson. Private Detective Mason Adler's angst at turning fifty is forgotten when his "birthday present," the handsome, young Henry Bowtrickle, turns up dead, and it's up to Mason to figure out who did it, and why. (978-1-63679-124-1)

Take Her Down by Lauren Emily Whalen. Stakes are cutthroat, scheming is creative, and loyalty is ever-changing in this queer, female-driven YA retelling of Shakespeare's Julius Caesar. (978-1-63679-089-3)

The Game by Jan Gayle. Ryan Gibbs is a talented golfer, but her guilt means she may never leave her small town, even if Katherine Reese tempts her with competition and passion. (978-1-63679-126-5)

Whereabouts Unknown by Meredith Doench. While homicide detective Theodora Madsen recovers from a potentially career-ending injury, she scrambles to solve the cases of two missing sixteen-year-old girls from Ohio. (978-1-63555-647-6)

Boy at the Window by Lauren Melissa Ellzey. Daniel Kim struggles to hold onto reality while haunted by both his very-present past and his never-present parents. Jiwon Yoon may be the only one who can break Daniel free. (978-1-63679-092-3)

Deadly Secrets by VK Powell. Corporate criminals want whistleblower Jana Elliott permanently silenced, but Rafe Silva will risk everything to keep the woman she loves safe. (978-1-63679-087-9)

Enchanted Autumn by Ursula Klein. When Elizabeth comes to Salem, Massachusetts, to study the witch trials, she never expects to find love—or an actual witch…and Hazel might just turn out to be both. (978-1-63679-104-3)

Escorted by Renee Roman. When fantasy meets reality, will escort Ryan Lewis be able to walk away from a chance at forever with her new client Dani? (978-1-63679-039-8)

Her Heart's Desire by Anne Shade. Two women. One choice. Will Eve and Lynette be able to overcome their doubts and fears to embrace their deepest desire? (978-1-63679-102-9)

My Secret Valentine by Julie Cannon, Erin Dutton, & Anne Shade. Winning the heart of your secret Valentine? These award-winning authors agree, there is no better way to fall in love. (978-1-63679-071-8)

Perilous Obsession by Carsen Taite. When reporter Macy Moran becomes consumed with solving a cold case, will her quest for the truth bring her closer to Detective Beck Ramsey or will her obsession with finding a murderer rob her of a chance at true love? (978-1-63679-009-1)

Reading Her by Amanda Radley. Lauren and Allegra learn love and happiness are right where they least expect it. There's just one problem: Lauren has a secret she cannot tell anyone, and Allegra knows she's hiding something. (978-1-63679-075-6)

The Willing by Lyn Hemphill. Kitty Wilson doesn't know how, but she can bring people back from the dead as long as someone is willing to take their place and keep the universe in balance. (978-1-63679-083-1)

Three Left Turns to Nowhere by Nathan Burgoine, J. Marshall Freeman, & Jeffrey Ricker. Three strangers heading to a convention in Toronto are stranded in rural Ontario, where a small town with a subtle kind of magic leads each to discover what he's been searching for. (978-1-63679-050-3)

Watching Over Her by Ronica Black. As they face the snowstorm of the century, and the looming threat of a stalker, Riley and Zoey just might find love in the most unexpected of places. (978-1-63679-100-5)

#shedeservedit by Greg Herren. When his gay best friend, and high school football star, is murdered, Alex Wheeler is a suspect and must find the truth to clear himself. (978-1-63555-996-5)

Always by Kris Bryant. When a pushy American private investigator shows up demanding to meet the woman in Camila's artwork, instead of introducing her to her great-grandmother, Camila decides to lead her on a wild goose chase all over Italy. (978-1-63679-027-5)

Exes and O's by Joy Argento. Ali and Madison really only have one thing in common. The girl who broke their heart may be the only one who can put it back together. (978-1-63679-017-6)

One Verse Multi by Sander Santiago. Life was good: promotion, friends, falling in love, discovering that the multi-verse is on a fast track to collision—wait, what? Good thing Martin King works for a company that can fix the problem, right…um… right? (978-1-63679-069-5)

Paris Rules by Jaime Maddox. Carly Becker has been searching for the perfect woman all her life, but no one ever seems to be just right until Paige Waterford checks all her boxes, except the most important one—she's married. (978-1-63679-077-0)

Shadow Dancers by Suzie Clarke. In this third and final book in the Moon Shadow series, Rachel must find a way to become the hunter and not the hunted, and this time she will meet Ehsee Yumiko head-on. (978-1-63555-829-6)

The Kiss by C.A. Popovich. When her wife refuses their divorce and begins to stalk her, threatening her life, Kate realizes to protect her new love, Leslie, she has to let her go, even if it breaks her heart. (978-1-63679-079-4)

The Wedding Setup by Charlotte Greene. When Ryann, a big-time New York executive, goes to Colorado to help out with her best friend's wedding, she never expects to fall for the maid of honor. (978-1-63679-033-6)

Velocity by Gun Brooke. Holly and Claire work toward an uncertain future preparing for an alien space mission, and only one thing is for certain, they will have to risk their lives, and their hearts, to discover the truth. (978-1-63555-983-5)

Wildflower Words by Sam Ledel. Lida Jones treks West with her father in search of a better life on the rapidly developing American frontier, but finds home when she meets Hazel Thompson. (978-1-63679-055-8)